A DEATH
IN A TOWN

NOVELS BY HILLARY WAUGH

Madam Will Not Dine Tonight
Hope to Die
The Odds Run Out
Last Seen Wearing . . .
A Rag and a Bone . . .
Rich Man, Dead Man . . .
The Eighth Mrs. Bluebeard
The Girl Who Cried Wolf
Sleep Long, My Love
Road Block
That Night It Rained
Murder on the Terrace
The Late Mrs. D.
Born Victim
Death and Circumstance
Prisoner's Plea
The Missing Man
End of a Party
Girl on the Run
Pure Poison
The Con Game
"30" Manhattan East
Run When I Say Go
The Young Prey
Finish Me Off
The Shadow Guest
Parrish for the Defense
A Bride for Hampton House
Madman at My Door
The Glenna Powers Case
The Doria Rafe Case
The Billy Cantrell Case
The Nerissa Claire Case
The Veronica Dean Case
The Priscilla Copperwaite Case
Murder on Safari

A DEATH IN A TOWN

HILLARY WAUGH

Carroll & Graf Publishers, Inc.
New York

First Carroll & Graf edition 1989

Carroll & Graf Publishers, Inc.
260 Fifth Avenue
New York, NY 10001

Library of Congress Cataloging-in-Publication Data

Waugh, Hillary.
    A death in town / Hillary Waugh.
        p.   cm.
    ISBN 0-88184-525-6 : $15.95
    PS3573.A9D4   1989
813'.54—dc20   89-10041
                                                       CIP

Manufactured in the United States of America

To Dick and Hope Whitehead . . .
In Appreciation

Thursday May 7

The last day of pretty sixteen-year-old Sally Anders' life began much as any other. She lazed in bed the customary five minutes after her mother's seven-o'clock knock and lost out to her thirteen-year-old brother in a dash for the bathroom. But let her mother tell about it.

JANE ANDERS

I didn't know, of course, what was going to happen later. I suppose I'd have treated her differently. But you always expect you'll see your children again—at bedtime, the next day, next year, the rest of your life.

She squabbled with Chris over the bathroom. She was always doing that, staying in bed till the last minute, then expecting to preempt the bathroom to dress and primp and get ready for school. She'd complain that Chris took too much time in there, that he'd make her miss the bus. And he'd complain that if she got there first, he wouldn't have time enough to wash his face. [It was a daily routine. You know how children are.] Not that Sally was that much of a child anymore. She was a junior in high school and had been invited to the senior prom. It was Ted Greaves invited her—Bill and Dorothy's son. Nothing against Sally, but personally I think they made him invite her. After all, she was only a junior, and they weren't going together or anything. He took her to the movies twice, that's all. I mean, Sally was a nice girl, but she didn't have what I'd call sex appeal. She was rather plain-looking. The newspapers all call her pretty—you know, "pretty sixteen-year-old Sally Anders," that sort of thing. But newspapers call all young women "pretty." I mean, Sally was nice-looking and all that, but I wouldn't regard her as a raving beauty. I told her that. She'd stand in front of the mirror and fuss with her hair and study her face, and I'd tell her there was only so much one could do about one's looks, that the thing to do to attract the boys was to develop a beautiful soul. The soul was something one could do something about.

Her hair, for example. It was that nondescript blond color that's between blond and brunette. She used to lighten it, to make herself look blond. I didn't want her doing that, but I couldn't watch her every minute. I have a job myself. Librarian at the high school. Besides, she had a mind of her own and sometimes it's just too much trouble trying to deal with her.

But about that day—Thursday, May seventh, a date you just don't ever forget, a date you can't think of without a knife stabbing your heart—Chris, as I say, got to the bathroom first, and he took his time in there. I think part of it was spite. Not that they weren't fond of each other, and I know that now, after what happened to his sister, he's sorry, but siblings do tend to pick on each other.

I was making breakfast. Jim, that's my husband, was already in his chair, reading the paper over his toast and coffee. He's always been an early riser. He has the chair with its back to the window where he gets the most light. He doesn't want to admit he ought to wear glasses, so he gets where the light is good.

Then Chris came in. I guess it was twenty after seven, and he took his seat. That's on Jim's right, facing the stove. He said, "Hi, Pop," which was the way he usually greeted his father. I don't like him calling Jim "Pop" and have told him that over and over, but Jim won't back me up and reinforce my position. He leaves everything to me. He thinks child-raising is woman's work and it's enough for him if he brings home a decent paycheck at the end of the week. He's an executive with Armour Rubber, head of Personnel, and he does all right, but there're a lot of people in town—a lot of them our friends, too—who earn a lot more than he does. We're struggling more than he wants to admit.

Chris said, "Hi, Pop," and Jim just grunted. He didn't even look up from the paper. Then Chris wanted to see the sports section and Jim handed it over. Chris wanted to know how the Red Sox made out. Jim was a Yankee fan because Joe DiMaggio was the first ballplayer he ever heard about. I used to have to listen to that sort of thing when he and I first started going together. Now he knows better than to try to talk baseball to me. Chris is the one he should get off on baseball with. But he's not interested in baseball anymore. He listens to Chris go on about the Red Sox, but the players are just names to him nowadays.

Sally came downstairs about twenty-five after seven. She was wearing the cotton print we picked out together at Stella's, which is the exclusive shop on the Green. Sally insisted on Stella clothes and would rather do without than wear anything from somewhere else. Girls today don't have any sense of thrift. They just want to impress the boys.

But it was a cute dress, I will say, and she looked very nice in it, for she did have a nice figure. Girls are at their best at sixteen and seventeen even if they aren't gorgeous. At least they're wholesome.

But that's the curse of being female and young. Even plain girls catch a man's eye. Sex is a very ugly thing and no one knows where its ugliness will strike. You wouldn't think it could touch a quiet, nice, well-brought-up, inno-

cent kind of girl like Sally. Veronica Struthers—yes. She
has the figure, the looks, the personality. Why couldn't it
have happened to Veronica Struthers? Girls like her are
just asking for trouble. She's not just a cheerleader type,
she's *the* cheerleader type. I've seen her prance on the
football field between the halves. It was when we played
Madison High and she was in that tight, form-fitting span-
gled costume that rode so high in back it all but revealed
her fanny, and was so low-cut in front you knew she
couldn't be wearing anything underneath. And she went
around, leading the other cheerleaders and the band,
thrusting her baton at the sky and lifting her knees so
high, and loving it. Oh, how she was loving it! And
I was thinking then, that she was asking for trouble.
Oh, boy, was she asking for trouble. I was going to
say that to Jim. We were at the game with the McKinleys.
Ordinarily we don't go to high-school football games,
but their son Hank was playing and they were having a
party after for some of the young people and some of
their parents.

I don't remember the game, but I do remember Veronica Struthers strutting around the field, showing off just
about everything she had, and just begging for trouble.
And I was going to say to Jim that the Struthers girl was
just asking for it—inviting it, even—but Jim, he was
staring at her, mesmerized. He was taken in by her just
the way she meant the men to be taken in. There wasn't
any point in telling him what a strumpet she was. He was
cheering her on. That's what he was doing.

So why wasn't it Veronica Struthers? Why did it have to
be a plain Jane like Sally who'd never catch anybody's eye
in a crowd? I saw Veronica the other day. She was at the
funeral with all the rest of the high-school student body. I
didn't notice the others, except the boys and girls I knew—
Sally's friends—but I did notice her. Even at a funeral,
even dressed demurely in black, even all sober-faced with
tear streaks on her cheeks, she stood out. And I thought
of how she was, last fall, in her minicostume on the
football field, arching her back till it would break, lifting

her knees to the sky. And I looked at her and all I could
think of was, Why wasn't it you? Why wasn't it you?

But that last breakfast—Sally didn't know anything was
going to happen to her later on. It was just another
breakfast—cereal, her favorite was 40% Bran Flakes, but
we were out and I gave her Rice Krispies. She said, "Aw,
Mom." I told her we were out of Bran Flakes. She said
she didn't like Rice Krispies and wanted cornflakes. I
said I didn't know she didn't like the Rice Krispies
and I'd already poured them so she could eat them this
once. She balked, and I looked at Jim. Daughters need
a father's firm hand if they're going to obey. If he told
her to eat what was set in front of her, she'd do it
without any fuss. But he just read his paper, and what
could I do? If I'd asked him to say something, I knew
what it'd be. He'd say, "Why can't she have what she
wants?"

So she got what she wanted anyway. I wasn't going
to argue. And I'm glad I didn't. I wouldn't want her
last day to be worse than it was. I'd like to think
that, until what happened to her happened, she'd been
happy.

Jim went off to work then. He gave Sally a kiss, mussed
Chris's hair, and bussed me, and that was that. Sally was
gobbling down her food and skimming the amusement
section of the paper. "Oh cripes," she said. "It's the
last day for—" and she mentioned one of those horror
movies the young people are so interested in. Then she
jumped to the phone to call Peggy Bodine about that.
Sally was baby-sitting at the Parkers' that evening, and
there was no way she and Peggy could manage the
movie together. They'd expected to see it the following
night.

I told her to finish her breakfast, that she could talk
to Peggy on the bus or in school, and she cut the con-
versation short. Even so, she left half her cereal when
she grabbed her books and went off. She gave me a kiss
and said "Bye" to Chris, and he reminded her he
wanted a high-school sticker to paste on his notebook.

He's only in eighth grade but will be entering high school in the fall.

Then she was gone, for her bus left before Chris has to go. And that was the last I saw of her until dinner.

Thursday May 7

JIM ANDERS

You don't think it can happen—not to you. Not to her. I wonder what she was thinking at the end. I don't sleep much anymore for wondering.

She was a sweet kid. Average, I suppose you'd call her—five feet four and a half, always wishing she had an extra three inches. Kids are so tall these days. I was tall in my day, looked down on most of my friends. Now their sons look down on me.

She was pretty, too. Nothing special, of course. You wouldn't call her beautiful. Even I wouldn't say that about her. But she was nice-looking, with a fresh, open expression, blondish hair, and a splash of freckles she didn't want—she tried more different creams and ointments to make them fade away—I guess she fell for every antifreckle advertising gimmick that hit television.

Her mother thinks Sally was a wallflower. Not me. Maybe boys didn't flock around her, but they didn't avoid her, either. She had friends of both sexes, but I think the

boys thought of her more as a pal or sister than as a
sweetheart. But that doesn't make her unpopular. She
had lots of girlfriends.

Not that she didn't worry and think she wasn't popular.
You know how young people are—basically insecure.

I don't know that I can tell you much about that day.
She was at breakfast, but I didn't pay much attention. To
tell you the truth, things aren't all that great between my
wife and me. We had children with the idea that they
would keep us together. Well, I guess they did that all
right, for that's the way we are right now—together. But
we aren't together, either. It's nobody's fault. We aren't
all that well suited.

However, that's not the subject right now. The reason I
don't remember much about that last breakfast is that it
was no different from a thousand other breakfasts. Sally
and Chris squabbled a lot. That's par for the course, I
guess. They didn't mean anything by it. Down deep they
really cared for each other. They were just damned if they
were going to let it show. Actually, they were getting
better. There was the morning bathroom fight, but the
rest of the time the friction had quieted down a lot, at
least as far as I could tell. Sometimes, they might even
favor each other with a kindness. Three or four years ago,
when Sally was entering her teens and Chris was a spunky,
self-assured ten-year-old, it seemed as if they couldn't say
two polite words to each other.

Of course, he still teased her. He was great at teasing.
And Sally was so sensitive. He could really get to her—
dissolve her in tears sometimes, ridiculing her about her
desire to be attractive. He knew where she was vulnerable.

So there was nothing special about this breakfast. I ate
my cereal and drank my coffee and read my paper. I use
the paper as a shield. If I hide behind the paper, I can
pretend I don't hear my wife. I can keep out of the family
conflicts, which, to tell you the truth, I think she gener-
ates. If she'd leave everybody alone, everything would
go like a clock. She's always after the kids about something, and after me to back her up. Don't hound them

so much is my motto. Don't ride such herd on them. They're okay.

But I guess that's off the subject, too. What I'm trying to say is that I have a tough job. I'm personnel director of one of the largest companies in this area, and what with union problems and unemployment problems and layoff problems and worker efficiency and staying competitive in today's market, I simply can't involve myself with the question of what time did Sally get home from her movie date last night, or why Chris didn't get his science paper in on time.

That's why I hide behind the paper at breakfast. Because Jane is so determined to get me involved. We had children so we could stay together. I think she wanted children so she could have something to worry about. I don't think she worries about anything else. The Armour Rubber Company could fall apart tomorrow, for all she knows. I could get fired tomorrow.

If I did, would I go to her? Of course not. I don't know who I'd go to. Maybe my brother. But he lives in California. He's got a lot of money—probably because he never married—but all we hear from him is a Christmas card signed by his secretary.

So what could I do if the ax falls? And there've been times when it's come close. I'm not indispensable, and I'm not untouchable, despite my seniority. I have nearly twenty years in with the company, and I'm only forty-six years old.

And now Sally's dead. I'm not used to it yet. I keep expecting—hoping—wanting—God, what a fool I am—to hear her squabble with Chris over bathroom rights just one more morning. I'd really listen that time—to the sound and inflection of her voice, to the way her tone would keen a little on the name "Chris" when she started getting frantic.

I don't know how my wife's painted me, but I'm not a heartless wretch. I did—I do—love that girl dearly. It seems incredible to me that someone could so callously have taken her life. She was so bright, so kind, so giving—so special.

Thursday May 7

CHRISTOPHER ALLEN ANDERS

I don't want to talk about it. I didn't mean to take over the bathroom. She could have the damned bathroom all day long if she wanted. I could use my friend Pete's bathroom. I practically live at his house anyway. His folks wouldn't mind.

What I mean is, there wasn't anything wrong with Sally. She was my sister. Maybe I didn't think about her as a girl, or a student, or a "date." I haven't had a date yet. Well, a bunch of us in the Hi-Y club had a dance and some of us guys brought girls—I mean our parents brought us guys and the girls to the dance, and drove us home again. And I *did* go with Frances Udack. But that's not a date, really, even if my mother made my father drive us to the YMCA and home again when it was over.

I didn't want for Sally to get killed. Maybe we had our fights and things, but that doesn't mean I didn't like her or wanted anything bad to happen to her—especially what *did* happen. If I'd been there, I wouldn't have let it happen. I wouldn't let anybody do anything to my sister, not while I had breath in my body.

But I wasn't there. I don't even know exactly what happened there. Nobody will tell me. All the grown-ups, including my father, say I'm too young. But I hear things from other people. My friends try to pretend they don't want me to know the latest scoop on accounta she was my sister. But that's not going to make her come alive again, and I want to know everything. I want to see the person who killed her burn in hell forever. And if I can find out who it is, I'll tell God and make Him send him there.

People want to know about that last day. People want to know what we ate for breakfast, what she was wearing, what everybody said, even what time she went to school. What difference does it make? That had nothing to do with her dying.

I think she had cornflakes with cut-up bananas for breakfast. That's what Mom gave me, I think. And Sally would have had coffee. She was great for coffee. Mom and Dad wouldn't let me have coffee for breakfast. Mom said it would stunt my growth, and Dad didn't say anything. Now, since Sally's dead, I'm allowed to have coffee for breakfast. If you can make anything out of that, I can't. I can't make anything out of anything, if you really want to know. For instance, what's God like? He does all of these things. He invented the universe, and He makes everything in the universe do what He wants. Except man. We don't do what He wants. Why doesn't He make us?

And what did Sally ever do to offend Him? I mean, why should she die? So, maybe she wasn't the Virgin Mary, but what of it? She was okay. I couldn't have had a better sister. I'm sorry I teased her. I didn't really mean to hurt her and make her cry. I don't know why I did it even.

Except she kind of let herself in for it. I don't quite know how to explain. Something about the way she'd sit, or look, or talk, or do whatever, would make me want to prick the bubble, let her know she wasn't the greatest Wonder Woman who ever came down the pike.

Like when she'd be in the house with her girlfriends.

Like that pain, Peggy. And Laura. She was another dip. I mean, Sally was all right most of the time, but when the three of them got together they were all the time giggly and all talking at once in their high-pitched voices, and all the time, all they could talk about was Boys, Boys, Boys. Or it would be the greatest rock star, and they'd play the tapes up so loud you could hear it a mile away. But it was always a *guy* who had them swooning on the floor. I mean, there're some pretty good female rock singers too, you know. I can name you some. I mean, I listen too. I know the songs. But the way I listen isn't like the way Sally and Peggy and Laura would lie on the floor, dead and quivering. I like to sit in a chair with headphones on and close my eyes so I get nothing but music. I don't want to squirm and twitch and giggle and poke somebody with an elbow so they can see how "sent" I am.

Sally wasn't *really* goofy like that, except around Peggy and Laura. I mean, alone around the house, she was real calm and controlled. When she was alone, she'd listen to music the way I do, put one of those cushioned head-phones on her head, and sit in her room nice and quiet and do her homework and, all the while, be getting the beat.

Mom didn't want her watching TV or listening to music when she had homework to do. Sally wasn't supposed to draw a long breath on her own until all her responsibili-ties were out of the way. That's what Mom's been drum-ming into me, too. So, if you want to listen to rock while you're doing your homework, you *have* to wear head-phones. Even if we don't have homework, we wear head-phones when Mom and Pop are home. They don't like our kind of music, just the way, Pop once told me, his folks didn't like *his* kind of music. Mom and Pop say it's too loud, it'll disturb the neighbors. So the only time the rock tapes are turned up loud in our house is when—was when—Sally was home after school with her girlfriends and Mom and Pop were still at work.

I'm trying to remember about that day. It's funny how it gets all cloudy. You'd think every single solitary thing you did that day would shine in your mind and stay forever. But it doesn't. It's only what happened *after* that I'll never forget.

Before what happened, it was all very normal. I walked to school—the Middle School, where I go, takes about ten minutes to get to. It's up State Street, across Route 1, along North State to Church, then a hundred yards up Church, and there it is. The high school, where Sally went, is two, two and a half miles away, and she had to go by bus.

But I went to school, and if you want, I can tell you what my classes are, what their times are, and the names of my teachers. In most cases, I can tell you the names of at least half the people in each class—we take different courses, so not everybody's in the same classes all the time. But I think nobody cares about that. All anybody talks about and cares about is where Sally went and what she did, even though it has nothing to do with her dying.

The high school gets out ahead of the middle school. I get home around half past three, but her classes let out at 2:45 and she's usually either home with her girlfriends when I get in, or she's at one of their houses and home is empty. I mean, Mom gets through with the high-school library about half past three, but then she has school stuff, meetings or people to see, or whatever grown-ups have to do, and she usually isn't home until at least four-thirty or even five.

Sally wasn't home this day because of choir practice at the church. We go to the Episcopal Church in town and Sally's all hot for church stuff. She used not to be, like me, but the last couple of years she's gotten RELIGION and spends a lot of time at the church with choir and fellowship meetings and things like that. I think it's because of boys. I mean, some of those Youth things have boys in them. Not the choir. That's almost all grown-ups, and they all walk down the aisle in black robes on the Sunday services holding hymnals and singing, and she and Peggy Bodine are the only ones in it who aren't grown-ups. But Sally and Peggy like singing and they both have pretty good voices—I mean, not like Tina Turner or anybody like that, but Mr. Stallings, the church organist and choir director, isn't that fussy. He'll take almost anybody who's willing to attend rehearsals and walk down the aisle in a black robe and sit up in the chancel through the service. And Sally took a liking to that.

Other people say she was at choir rehearsal that afternoon so I guess nobody was home that day when I got back from school. I only know I dumped my books and things and biked over to Pete Herly's house. Pete's my best pal, and we were trying to set up a slot-car racing track. It doesn't matter.

What matters, I suppose, is I came home for supper and Sally was there and the four of us had our usual dinner, meaning we'd sit down at the table and have whatever it was that Mom served us—I can't say for sure what we ate that night, because it didn't matter that much. What happened was we'd sit down for dinner and all say grace, and there'd be the usual hassle. Mom would want to know what we kids—Sally and I were the kids—had been doing all day, and if we'd done our chores—tidied our rooms, spent some time on our homework, that sort of thing.

I remember Sally saying she hadn't done any homework. I think there was some talk about choir practice, that Mom thought it was interfering with Sally's homework, and Sally saying she'd do her homework while she baby-sat for the Parkers. The Parkers live on North Ferry Street, at the corner of Peach Lane, and they have two boys, a four-year-old, Richard, and a two-and-a-half-year-old named David. They were going to a concert in New Haven with some other people and wouldn't be back before midnight. I remember Sally had to gobble her food because she had to be there at seven o'clock, and there was a bit of a squabble—no worse than usual—about her eating too fast, and her complaining that dinner should have been served earlier.

Thursday May 7

We need to hear from Dorothy Meskill. She saw Sally that day. But first, let us listen to Ethelbert Stallings, director of the St. Bartholomew's Episcopal Church choir. Mr. Stallings has been choir director for fourteen years. He teaches organ and piano, and tunes pianos, both privately and for the Halston music firm in New Haven. Mr. Stallings' wife, Esther, does cleaning and dusting in the church and helps in the kitchen when suppers are served.

ETHELBERT STALLINGS

Thursday, May seventh? Oh, I won't forget that day! She was a very nice girl, that Sally Anders. She and Peggy Bodine. They behaved very properly in with the older women and men. The number of people in the choir ranges between twelve and sixteen. We have sixteen if everybody shows, but choir practice is one of those avocations that few people put ahead of everything else. There are four or five women—I'd say five—who won't let anything stand in the way of their participating in the Sunday service. I call them the reliables. Unfortunately, their voices aren't the equal of their dedication, but they are competent enough, and they try very hard. They understand their responsibility. A couple of the men are retired, and they can be counted on too. They don't have other things, like an occupation, getting in their way.

So we can count on a minimum of twelve voices on a Sunday. We get the whole sixteen about once a month. The rest of the time, there are problems of sickness, or being on vacation, or being called out of town. Sometimes, it's just having guests for the weekend; but there's not much of that. I long ago learned that constancy of purpose was a more valuable asset than a good singing voice if one wanted to build up a dependable choir.

Well, about this day. There wasn't anything special about it. Sally and Peggy came in about five minutes late. That was good for them. That's to say, most of the time they were late. Not late enough to matter, to make a fuss about. You might think, since they were the young ones in the group, that they'd be first to arrive, but, you see, they had really good voices. They had the best voices by far, male or female. And they knew music. Peggy and Sally had both studied piano. I think Sally said she was started on piano when she was five years old. she once told me she knew how to read music before she could read words. She had an aunt who was a piano teacher— lived in New Haven—who'd studied with Begall—Saul Begall in New York. And her mother had studied with Begall too. There was music in the family.

And Peggy'd had piano too—started when she was nine or ten. So, really, it didn't matter *when* they came in. They could pick up the music of whatever we were working on and sight-read it right off, and carry their parts. I could've practically given them the music out in the vestibule on Sunday morning and let 'em go. Not quite, of course. Even the best has to go over a piece a few times to learn the expression and proper blending with the other voices.

They sat together. They always did, though Peggy's

contralto and Sally was soprano. They liked doing part singing together. You could see them smile at each other when it was going right. They were listening to themselves really, not to the choir as a whole.

The rehearsal went well. A little trouble here and there. The Bach chorale was more difficult than I usually give the choir, quite demanding in fact, but it's a glorious piece and I felt they could handle it.

We got through a little after five and Mr. Wallace, the minister, stopped by the choir loft. He listened to the last few minutes of rehearsal and seemed pleased.

After that, I put the music away and picked up my things. And the others? They broke up and went on their way.

When I came down the stairs and looked into the church, Sally was talking to Mr. Wallace by the back pews, over on the other aisle. I was looking into the church to see if Esther—that's my wife—was inside. She does the cleanup work; vacuums the carpets there, and in the parish house next door, at the end of the driveway; helps with the suppers and the dishes. I don't think the church could function without her. The pay isn't great, but she enjoys the work. I was looking for her, as I say, for it was time to go home. Anyway, Sally and Mr. Wallace were talking together very seriously. I thought Sally looked a little upset about something. I don't know what they were talking about, and they didn't see me, but I didn't pay any attention. Sally's very into church these days and she talks to the minister a lot.

That's about all I can tell you about that day. Esther wasn't in there vacuuming. I forget where I found her—in the parish hall, or maybe downstairs in the church office or one of the Sunday School rooms.

When we got into the car, Mr. Wallace was crossing from the church to his home, the other side of the drive. He gave a smile and a wave and we drove out to the street. I thought Sally would be out there, heading for home with Peggy, but I didn't see either of them. Not that I was looking for them; I just half expected they wouldn't've got out of sight across the Green yet.

Thursday May 7

DOROTHY MESKILL

The thing I remember most about that day was the scare I got that morning. I don't scare easy, and I can't say I was really frightened, but for a while there, I had a very uneasy feeling. Edward and I live on North Ferry Street near the north end of Ogilvy Pond, maybe a hundred yards south of I-95, the Connecticut Turnpike, near the Crockford exit. It's close enough so you get the hum of traffic all the time and some of the trucks can be a real distraction. You get used to it, though. It's so you don't even notice.

The house isn't great. I mean, it's a nice house, and larger than it looks, and I can't complain. Edward teaches sociology in the high school, getting extra money as head of the drama club, and while teacher salaries are getting better, you aren't going to buy a yacht on them. But it's comfortable. We've been here three years now and are very happy with the environment. Crockford's a nice town to live in—lots of old homes dating from the Colonial period, mixed in with newer ones, some small and inexpensive, others nice and large, with land around. You'd be

18

amazed how big some of the backyards are, behind houses
that look cheek by jowl. I say you'll find rabbits raiding
vegetable gardens literally a stone's throw from the Green.

The Green is big—not as big as New Haven's, but one
of the biggest in New England. And, like most New England villages and towns, the Green's got stores and homes
around it, and churches. Churches: I don't think there's a
green anywhere that doesn't have at least one church
facing it. We have three. On the east side, on Green
Street, there's the Episcopal Church, adjoining the parking area for the town hall. Then, at the north end of the
Green, there's the Congregational Church, on the corner
of, you guessed it, Church Street. The Catholic Church is
on the west side of the Green, almost opposite the town
hall. That's the newest one. Red brick with white trim.
The old Catholic Church used to be a couple of blocks
down Whitney Street, a clapboard frame building with a
stained-glass window. I think the Elks Lodge has it now.

Where Ed and I live, on North Ferry Street, it's maybe a
half-mile to the Green. The road here is kind of secluded.
There're neighbors, especially down Siddons Street, which
splits off, but where we are, the homes are wider-spaced and
the bushes and trees separate you and it's kind of private.

So this morning, it was about ten o'clock. I got up with
Ed and we had our breakfast and he headed off in the car
for school. We only have one car and he takes it unless
there's something I'm going to need it for, like a dental
appointment or something else that I can't walk to. Then I
drive him to school and pick him up after. But that's a
pain and most of what I want to do in town is within
walking distance, or biking distance, and if it isn't, there's
usually a friend going along and she can pick me up. Like
if we play tennis over at the middle-school courts, I'll walk
over. It's not that far, but the women I play with live too
far away and, like as not, we'll drive to my place after for
iced tea and we can gab and relax.

But Thursday, May seventh, I wasn't playing tennis. I
was going to do some gardening. We have a fence out by
the road and I've been trying to train some rambler roses

to cover it, and have flower beds on the inside facing the house. So that's what I was doing at about ten o'clock that morning. I was wearing a pair of linen shorts that have seen their best days, old tennis sneakers without socks, a plaid blouse with a button missing down the front, a wide-brimmed straw hat, and I was down on my knees on a kneepad, my hands in work gloves, digging with a trowel and putting weeds and stuff into a basket.

I was in the middle of that, perspiring plentifully, but enjoying the work, when I had this sense of being watched. I looked up and there was a man close up on the street side of the fence looking down at me. He was young, with long brown hair, but the hair was unkempt and his face was unwashed. It had the appearance that he'd last rinsed it in the men's room of a fast-food emporium somewhere.

His clothes were dusty, too, as if he'd been a long time on the road. He was wearing a checked flannel shirt with long sleeves and he had a pair of dungarees on, and heavy hiking boots—I could see his shoes through the fence pickets. And, maybe because I was missing a button, I noticed that the right sleeve of his plaid shirt was torn.

I gasped when I looked up. To tell the truth, I almost shrieked. It wasn't just that I hadn't heard him approach and that I was caught by surprise, and it wasn't that he was a stranger, someone I'd never seen before, but there was something about his eyes, about the way he looked at you that was scary. It was as if he were looking at you through your clothes. I know they talk about men imagining what a woman would look like if she weren't wearing anything, and they may do it as much as some of the psychiatrists and psychologists says, but if you're a woman, most of the time you're not aware that they're doing it to you. At least, if they do, it either doesn't show in their eyes, or, if it would show, they do it when you're looking the other way.

With this man, though, there was something bold and frank about his eyes and the way they looked at you. You know, I'm in my mid-thirties and this young man couldn't have been over twenty-five, but the way he looked at me made me extremely self-conscious: about the fact that my

legs were bare, and especially about that missing button
on my shirt. I was wearing a brassiere, of course. I'd never
go out of the house without one, even into my own yard.
But the look in his eye made me want to feel the catch in
front to make sure I had it on—except that that was right
where he was looking, just as bold as you could believe.

I said, "Oh!" and he grinned and said he didn't mean to
startle me, but he was new in town, had just got off the
turnpike, and did I know where Williams Street was?

I was rather flustered, and I stood up and said I didn't
know of any Williams Street. He said he was looking for a
family named Durham on Williams Street, and all the
while he was—well, the only way to describe it is—
looking me over.

I said I couldn't help him, so then he suggested that
maybe I could look them up in the phone book, for it was
important that he get in touch with them.

I didn't want to turn my back on him, to tell the truth.
And I didn't want anything more to do with him, but I
didn't know what to say. I felt put on a spot. He hadn't
done anything to me, threatened me or anything, so I
couldn't very well be impolite. He might have been telling the truth for all I knew. So I said I'd go look, and I
turned and headed into the house. I left the door open to
let him know I'd be right back, but he apparently took it
as a different kind of invitation, because I was no sooner at
the phone book beside the phone in the kitchen than I
found him right behind me.

I was just picking up the book, and to have him walk
into the house without a by-your-leave was extremely
angering. I wanted to tell him to get out immediately,
except that he was so big and so close to me I thought—
well, I don't know *what* I thought, except I guess I
imagined him raping me and robbing the house. My
knees turned completely to water and my throat went dry
and I couldn't utter a word. I just held the book half
opened.

What he did was smile and look around and say, "Nice
place you've got here. You live alone?"

All I could say was "no" and fumbled through the pages of the phone book as fast as I could. And, of course, there was no Durham in the phone book and there's no Williams Street, either. I didn't think there was, and I checked the street map later to make sure.

So when I told him that, he looked me over in that way he had, and looked round again as if there might be a bedroom handy. Well, I didn't give him a chance to say anything more. I said, "I'm sorry, you must have the wrong address," and I pushed past and got to the open door where at least I could scream with some chance of being heard if he didn't leave.

But he didn't make any fuss. He came right along and out the house and looked around at the other houses and the scenery and, back at the fence, he went through the gate and smiled at me again and thanked me very nicely and said he was sorry to bother me and, yes, he probably had the wrong name, or maybe it was the wrong town.

Then, though, instead of heading back the way he'd come, to I-95, he went the other way, toward Siddons Street and the way to town. I know all that has nothing to do with Sally Anders, and you want to hear about the last time I ever set eyes on her, but what happened with that strange, tall young man with those threatening eyes left me shaken the whole rest of the morning. It affected my whole day. I didn't really want to work in the garden anymore. I put away the things and took a long bath and made some lunch. But all that while, I was wondering where he'd gone and debating whether I should notify the police or not.

About one o'clock, that's what I decided I should do. The man's story was so patently made up, and from the way he looked around at the house, the television and all, I'm sure he was sizing the place up as a place to rob. He might've been scouting for a band of thieves who'd come along later. And I think, with the slightest bit of encouragement, he'd have been taking off my clothes. I couldn't get over the feeling I'd had a narrow escape.

So I phoned the police. I'd never done that before, phoned the police department. But the lieutenant, Lieutenant

Hanlon, was very nice and didn't laugh at me. He listened
very soberly and asked exactly when it had happened, and
for a description, and then he asked why I'd waited so
long to telephone. I didn't know that it mattered, but he
said if I'd called right away, a police car could have
intercepted him and asked him what he wanted.

But to get back to Sally, I attended a church membership committee meeting in the parish house at four. I'm
chairman, and there are five of us, two other women and
two men. That lasted until about five, and when we were
breaking up and I was getting into the car—which I use
once Edward gets home from school—I saw Sally and
Peggy coming out from the church and I gave them a
ride. They both live on State Street just off the Green and
frankly, I didn't expect they'd be interested, but they
wanted to go to Ferguson's, the shoe and clothing store on
Route 1, and it was on my way.

Now I'm supposed to tell you anything special about
their behavior, because of what happened later. But there
wasn't anything, really, at least that I noticed. Peggy was
going to buy a pair of shoes and Sally was going with her
and they were talking about a movie Peggy was going to,
but Sally couldn't because she had a baby-sitting job that
night. It was at the Parkers', I remember her saying. She
said she'd be putting the children to bed and doing homework while Peggy would be at the movie having all the
fun. And she asked if some boy—and I'm sorry, I don't
remember the name—would be there. And I can't tell
you whether the boy was someone Sally was interested in,
or a special friend of Peggy's. Sorry about that.

But I don't think that's what's important, if you want
my opinion. After what happened to Sally, I can't get my
mind off that strange and frightening man who startled me
by my fence. I'm not saying he had anything to do with
anything. I don't know where he went after I saw him.
Nor do the police, the last I heard. But what happened to
Sally has never happened in this town before, so I have to
look to what's been going on that's different.

Thursday May 7

PAMELA PARKER

Sally Anders had been baby-sitting for us for two years, since she was fourteen. We'd had a couple of baby-sitters before her, of course, since Richard's four now. David's two and a half and he doesn't remember any other baby-sitter. Well, of course, now and then Sally wouldn't be available and we'd have to have someone else, but David doted on Sally. She played with him and gave him lots of hugs. She loved babies. She liked all children, but she was particularly fond of babies. I remember the first time she came to sit for us. David was a tiny thing in his carriage. It was afternoon and we, Charlie and I, were going to a picnic. It was a Republican fund-raising outing, where someone supplies the lawn and the party faithful pour drinks for the guests, and the wives provide the hors d'oeuvres and sandwiches and cakes and coffee and goodies, and all that. Charge ten bucks a head or fifteen a couple, and, outside of the cost of the liquor and setups and mailings, it's practically all profit. Charlie's active in the party—in fact, he's on the Police Commission—so, naturally, we went. In fact, I deviled a couple dozen eggs for the occasion.

It was just about the first time we were to leave David with a sitter. Richard, of course, being older, was used to them. Sally arrived, up from State Street which is no more than a five- to ten-minute walk. I saw her come off the road onto the semicircular gravel drive we've got out front because the house is set back quite a bit from the road. She had pigtails back then, and she was wearing a plaid skirt, cotton blouse, and a little blue jacket, and she was skipping and happy and her pigtail was bouncing, and I couldn't help thinking what a pretty picture she made. It was her first time sitting for us, but we'd known her since she was a toddler, through the church, for one thing, and we socialized with her folks, traveled in the same circle, you know.

She came in and I took her out onto the patio where David was in the carriage and I remember her gazing at him, lying under his blanket with only his face showing, and there was awe in her eyes, as if babies were the rarest things in the world, and she asked if she could hold him. So I picked him up, which woke him, and he started to cry, but the moment Sally had him in her arms, cradled against her shoulder, rocking him and crooning, he stopped instantly. I have to say, she could quiet David much faster than I could. She had a way with her. I think, when I saw that, I decided Charles and I had picked ourselves a permanent baby-sitter. We hoped she wouldn't outgrow the need or the desire before the children got old enough to be left on their own.

But, of course, it's the night of May seventh you want to know about. It was a Thursday and so ordinary your mind doesn't trap any of the things that go on—until after, when you find out that the day wasn't ordinary. Then you find yourself wracking your brain trying to recall what, of that day, was significant, what was different, or odd about that one time. And I can't think of anything odd. Not until we came home.

Let me tell it to you as best I can. We were going to the

concert with the Whitesides. Faith and Bill. At Woolsey Hall in New Haven. We four have had season tickets to the series for years, and customarily we meet at the Whitesides', who live just above us on the other side of Peach Lane, which goes up the hill beside our house. The concert starts at eight-thirty, so we like Sally to come at seven, which gives us time to walk up to the Whitesides' and the four of us drive from there. If we leave by seven-thirty, there's plenty of time to get to Woolsey Hall, find a parking place, and get to the concert in comfort. No rush, no fuss.

Sally was right on time. That was one of the nice things about Sally. In addition, not only did she love children and take good care of them—you'd never find her shutting herself off in the study, listening to rock music through headphones, oblivious to fire alarms, the telephone, the cries of the children. She always came with an armload of books, and after she saw to it that the children were tucked in, she settled down at the dining-room table, under the overhead light, which is very dim since it's electric candles for appearance, not for illumination, and did homework. When she was through with the homework, sometimes she'd read on the couch in the living room until we got home. I used to worry about her doing her homework, though, in such bad light. "You only have one pair of eyes," I'd tell her. "You ought to protect them."

But she always claimed she could see perfectly well in such light. To tell the truth, I have to put on glasses to read newspaper print under a bright lamp, but these young people. You can't tell them anything. They really think they know it all. I used to think to myself, You, my dear Sally, will be wearing thick-lensed glasses before you know it, and you'll wonder why.

But I was wrong. She never wore glasses and now she never will.

The concert was— Damned if I can remember now. There was Brahms, and a modern piece I didn't like, by someone I never heard of. They play the good stuff first,

like the Brahms. You can bet, before the intermission, it's
going to be Brahms or Beethoven, or someone like them—
the very best of the classical composers. Then, for the
second half, they play a discordant modern piece written,
I'm sure, by an inferior modern composer. You can be
certain his name isn't Hindemith, or one of those very
modern, but recognized composers. It's going to be by
someone strident and young, who's never been heard of
before, and never will be again. The Whitesides and we
agree it's a plot to put down modern music. They play the
best of the oldies and worst of the newies and say to the
audience, "Now, what have you got to say about modern
music?" We have to wonder what it would be like if they
played a symphony by an unknown nineteenth-century
composer and gave us Stravinsky or Shostakovich for a
taste of twentieth-century fare.

You may think that's off the subject, but, truthfully, I
don't recall the composers on the program, but that's what
we were talking about coming home afterward. Call Bill
and Faith. They'll have a copy of the program. They can
tell you exactly what was played.

As for us, the concert ended about ten-thirty, which
was the customary time. We all rode back to the Whitesides',
getting there about eleven. Charlie and I stayed for a glass
of wine, then walked down to our place. I wasn't keeping
track of the time, but I'd guess it was between eleven-
thirty and quarter of twelve.

Now this is what you want to know about. Everything
we felt and saw.

First of all, there're no lights on Peach Lane up on the
hill, so the moment we walk down the Whitesides' drive,
beyond reach of their floodlamps, we're in almost total
darkness until we get within range of the light on our
barn. From there, we can get down the slope of our yard
from the barn to the back light on the patio. So we carry a
flashlight if we go up to the Whitesides' in the dark. This
time we'd forgotten, since the sun was still up when we
were to leave for the concert.

We started out of their place and realized we had no

flash, so Faith ran back inside and brought us one. And we used that to guide us home, which, in a direct line, would be less than a hundred yards but, going out their drive and then back on Peach Lane to our barn and home, would be another fifty at least.

The first thing that struck us as not quite right, was when we were approaching the house. There was no light on the patio. In fact, we couldn't see any lights on at all. Sally was always careful about lights. She didn't turn on what she didn't need. She'd been brought up with the adage "Waste not, want not." When she was baby-sitting, the only rooms she used were the dining and living rooms, and she'd turn out the dining-room chandelier when she moved to the living room. The television was in the back room, behind the kitchen and laundry—the "gun room" we call it, because a previous owner exhibited his gun collection there—but she didn't look at our television. She felt she'd be too far away to hear the children. And besides, she almost always had homework to do.

But the back patio light was off, and the living room was dark. I remember saying to Charles, laughing, but a little puzzled, "What's she doing, taking a nap?"

"Power failure," Charles thought. Then he said, "But the barn light's on."

We found the patio door into the kitchen was wide open. The screen door was in place, of course, and wasn't locked. We don't lock up in our town. We haven't had to come to that yet, though maybe it's time to put locks on everything, don't leave the car in the drive without locking the doors, or in the shopping center. Don't go to the store without locking all the doors and windows.

It's come to that now, I guess, after what happened. Maybe I should have insisted that Sally keep the house locked while she was in it alone with the children. But *we* never did. Nobody in town did that sort of thing.

And now the back door to the kitchen was wide open. Charles went in first, throwing the switch, and the lights came on. There was no power failure. The lights had all been turned off.

I threw on the dining-room lights, leading the way. I was perturbed, and I was going to want an explanation. Charles, he was willing to let me go first. I don't think he knew how to make a complaint to her. She'd always been so agreeable and pleasant and young and nice. Men don't know what to do in the face of a young, innocent, vibrant girl. To tell the truth, I think all they see in her is sex. And when you face them with sex, they simply don't know how to handle it.

I wasn't going to be sharp with Sally. If I was surprised that she'd turned off all the lights, I was equally certain she'd have a perfectly rational explanation. I knew, with her in the house, no harm could come to the children and that, of course, was my first and only concern. To tell the truth, I wasn't even thinking about the children, whether they were all right or not. I *knew* they were. Sally would have seen to it. My only concern was why Sally had left the kitchen door wide open and turned off all the lights. What I'm saying is, if you're a mother, and you have a nest, a home that you care about, and you leave it, making sure, of course, that you put it in good hands, if you come back and see that "nest" in what appears to be an out-of-the-ordinary condition, your first concern is to find out what happened, then restore the "nest" to its proper state.

I went first into the living room, turning on the nearest lamp. Charles was following, and though I wasn't watching his face, I can tell you the expression. It was "pondering." Charles is a ponderer. He's not going to say, "Something's amiss! We must *act* immediately!" He's going to hem and haw and wonder what could have happened.

That's why I was leading the way. Because I wanted to know what Sally had been up to. I was uneasily wondering if she was a fit baby-sitter for our children.

Now I don't want you to get the idea I had any doubts about that. Not after two years. What I'm trying to say is that a woman's first response when she finds something unexpected is to lay blame. I was angry. Because I was disturbed.

First off, what I did when I found no one in the living room was to go through to the study, which is off the front entrance hall. The lights were off in there as well, and I could tell before I snapped them on that Sally wasn't there.

That's when I decided to check on the children. If she wasn't anywhere else, she had to be with them. So I hurried to their bedroom, which is on the first floor back of the living-room fireplace and staircase, across from the bath. We bunk them there and sleep in the master bedroom up off the head of the stairs. Richard has a single bed and David is still in the crib, and we keep the doors open so we can hear them.

Charles was with me by that time and followed me inside. The windows were open. I could feel the breath of flowing air when I turned on the light. I was sure Sally would be with them, that one of them had waked up and cried, and she'd dozed off beside them.

They were both safe and snug, thank God, both sound asleep, David with his thumb in his mouth. We haven't been able to break him of that yet.

But there was no sign of Sally. "What on earth?" I remember saying. "Where can she have gone?"

Charles went back out to the dining room. What I did was give both boys a kiss and straighten their sheets. You don't know the feeling of relief a mother gets, no matter what else may be going on, to know her children are safe. I closed their door, and when I returned, Charles was gesturing at Sally's books neatly piled on the dining table. "Her books are here," he said.

"But where is *she*?" I said. "I can't understand this."

Charles thought maybe she'd gone to one of the upstairs bedrooms to nap. I said she wouldn't do that. She wasn't the kind to go into rooms she wasn't supposed to. She'd never have gone through my dresser drawers or poked around in my jewelry box, for example. She was too respectful of other people's rights and property.

But Charles went up to see. He took the stairs two at a time, and I sensed he was beginning to become alarmed.

We have three bedrooms and a bath up there, plus my little room off the master bedroom, and there's a back spare room that overlooks the gun room and has a connecting staircase.

He went through them all, pretty fast, and then he called down, "She's not up here!"

"What'll we do?" I wanted to know when he raced back down. "Where could she be?"

All Charles did was shake his head. Then he decided to call the Anders, to see if she'd come home or if she'd told them what she was going to do.

He got hold of Jim Anders. Right now it was quarter of twelve. Jim said he didn't know anything. Sally wasn't home, that's all he knew. And he called Jane to the phone, but Jane didn't know anything either. She remembered something about Peggy Bodine going to a movie that evening but thought Sally had said she couldn't go with her because she had to baby-sit.

That was the only thing we could think of, that maybe she'd left the children and gone off to the movie with Peggy, planning to be back before we got home so she could pretend she'd been here all the time. Now, of course, that's not at all like Sally, but at a time like this, you realize how little you know about a person, especially a young teenager.

But if that's what she'd done, why wasn't she back? The only answer we could come up with was, perhaps there'd been an accident. We both agreed the whole scenario sounded pretty farfetched, but the Bodines were the only ones we could think of to telephone.

I thought the Anders ought to be the ones to make the call. After all, Sally was their daughter. But Charles felt a responsibility and he got hold of Marion Bodine and got to talk to Peggy who said, no, Sally hadn't gone to the movies, she'd had to baby-sit, and Peggy'd gone with Susan Bobbit and Dorothy Carlson.

Charles tried to call Jim Anders back but the line was busy. Then Jim phoned Charles. He'd talked to Peggy himself and heard just what we'd heard. So Jim and

Charles talked together in low, very serious tones, trying to decide what could've happened to Sally, what they should do to try to find her.

There wasn't much they could do. They talked about calling some of Sally's other friends, but it was midnight now and they didn't want to get people up who wouldn't know anything anyway. As Jim put it to Charles, if something had happened to Sally, whoever knew about it would be phoning *him*. It wouldn't be the other way around.

The trouble was, they couldn't think of anything else. They talked about places she might've gone to. They even wondered if she might have gone to a bar. But that was just plain silly, imagining Sally trying to pick up men at a bar!

Finally, Charles suggested they call the police. Jim thought that was the only thing left to do. Charles offered to call them, because he's on the Police Commission and if he told them to look into it, they'd do it. But Jim wanted to make the call since it was his daughter, and he said he'd report back. I remember thinking, when Charles hung up, that it was five minutes past twelve and Sally should have been home in bed by now.

Friday May 8

CHARLES PARKER

Jim called me back at quarter past twelve. I was out in
the kitchen making Pam and me a cup of instant coffee.
Right then I was pretty wound up. I don't know that I was
really worried about Sally. You know how those things
are, something strange happens and you can't imagine
what brought it about. And more often than not, you
blame the person because you think there's no possible
way the person could justify what happened. And then
the person shows up with a very simple explanation which
answers everything, and it's the one explanation you never
thought of.

So I kept expecting Sally would telephone with some
perfectly rational reason for running off and leaving the
children. Except that I couldn't think of one.

To tell the truth, when Jim phoned, I answered feeling
almost sure he was going to say Sally was home and
everything was fine. I half expected George McCrory,
who had the night duty, would tell him she'd fallen down-

stairs and broken a leg or something and the police had
taken her to the hospital. I know that sounds ridiculous—
doing that and not leaving word. That's not the way we
run the police department. But I had my fingers crossed
that the force had goofed up in some way.

Instead, Jim was very, very sober. I don't think I'd ever
heard him speak so slowly and quietly and yet with a
special note in his voice, which said he'd never been in
such a situation before and he was scared to death. What I
mean is, he didn't even try to reassure me that everything
would be all right. I could sense he was sure everything
was not all right, that something very serious had happened to Sally, that she'd been kidnapped or something.

That's because Sergeant McCrory hadn't heard anything about anybody being missing, or anybody having
any kind of emergency. Instead, he listened very carefully
and took down the information and said he'd alert the
patrol cars and pass the word.

I told Jim I was sure they'd find her very quickly once
the word got out, that she couldn't have gone far. Then I
phoned George myself and wanted to know what he
thought.

George didn't have any particular ideas. He said he
asked Mr. Anders about her wanting to run away, about
any boys she might have been involved with, about drugs.
Mr. Anders denied all of those things, but George was
pretty sure it was drugs. He didn't pursue it with Anders,
he said, because all he'd get was denials. Parents are
usually the last ones to find out what their children are up
to, George said, and he asked me what I knew. I hadn't
heard of her being involved in drugs and, frankly, neither
had the police, and they have a line on most of the kids in
town who're involved. Then he told me one thing that he
was a little worried about. There'd been two reports of a
stranger being seen in town. One was from Dorothy Meskill,
who lives only two or three hundred yards from us up
North Ferry Street. She reported the stranger around one
o'clock, about being disturbed by his appearance and manner, but said that he forked left down Siddons Street

rather than our way down North Ferry. But he might well have come back by our house later and been tempted to burgle it.

The other report came from Millie Stone on State Street. She'd found the same man in her backyard, and when she asked him what he wanted, he said he was looking for a man named Durham who was supposed to live at that address. She told him to leave, but he was slow and insolent about it, and when he did leave, it was over her back fence into the rear yard of the Fowler property which fronts on Church Street. She phoned a complaint to the police ten minutes later, at two-forty, and a patrol car was on the lookout for him around the area of the Green, but he wasn't to be seen.

George noted that the Anders live on State Street and that the stranger might have seen Sally at some point that afternoon and started following her. There was no evidence that this happened, of course, and if she'd been taken from our house by force, there should be some evidence. That's what George thought, and he called Detective Harris in on the case and had him come up to look around.

Friday May 8

DETECTIVE JACK HARRIS

Sarge called me—Sergeant McCrory—at half past twelve according to the blotter. I was taking a shower. Ethel, that's my wife, was asleep. I keep the bathroom door open when the water's running, because you never know, in my business, what hour of the day or night that phone's gonna ring.

I answered, and the Sarge briefed me. Sally Anders was missing.

I know Sally—I know who she is. It's a small town and a small high school and my daughter Katie's a year behind her. Sally was in a school play last year. She played "Laurie" in *Oklahoma!*. Good, too!

That's off the subject. I got this call she was missing and I got this gut feeling. I don't know how to explain it. I'm no fortune-teller and I don't believe in ESP or "vibrations" or any of that stuff, but I had this sinking feeling. Probably it's because I've been a cop so long. All I know is, a shudder went through me and I thought to myself,

36

This is *bad!* It's one of those things. When something goes wrong with certain people, you know it's nothing to worry about. It's a fact of their lives and they'll come up smelling like roses. And then there are other people, and you know that nothing goes wrong in *their* lives. And when you hear something *is* wrong, you *know* the worst has happened. Don't tell me how, you just *know* it. If they don't get home on time, you *know* it's not because they went out on a bender, or they had a secret girlfriend someplace. You know they ran into a tree, or got hit by a drunk-driver, or got robbed, or raped and murdered. Because otherwise, they'd be home when they were supposed to be.

And Sally Anders was one of those people.

I got dressed as fast as I could, and woke Ethel to tell her I had to go out. She was drowsy and didn't ask why. She learned a long time ago not to ask why—if she wants to go back to sleep.

And I didn't tell her. I just said the Sarge called and I had to report. I didn't even say "accident," because she wouldn't decide it was a tractor-trailer turned over on I-95, she'd figure, at this hour, five drunk teenagers had wrapped their old man's car around a tree, and how many were still alive.

I didn't go to headquarters, I drove to the Parkers'. The car clock said 12:45 and I put that in my logbook. I always like to record times and names of people.

It looked like every light in the house was on. Even the lone house across the road, where old Mrs. Tyler lives, had lights. The Anders' Lincoln and one of our patrol cars were in the drive in front and Mr. Parker was out on the stoop, waiting.

I took the steps two at a time and he grabbed my hand. "Thank God you're here," he said. "Maybe you can make some sense out of this."

Inside, in the living room, was patrolman Gary Little, Mrs. Parker, the Anders, the Whitesides, and old, white-haired, deaf Mrs. Tyler. The little Parker children were up, too, Richard and David, and Gary was asking them where Sally had gone. Richard was rubbing his eyes and David was crying. Mrs. Tyler grabbed my arm and said she wished she could help, but she didn't know anything until Mr. Parker had banged on her door.

Gary said the children didn't remember anything. Mr. Parker showed me Sally's books, neatly stacked on the dining table. He didn't think she'd done any studying.

I asked if any search had been made. They said they'd looked around the yard and in the barn, and they'd called her name. Gary said police cars were patrolling the roads. Mr. Parker suggested we call Ray Hunter up at the north end of town. He keeps dogs and had a bloodhound who might track her. I said it was worth a try. Frankly, I didn't see much point in it, but everybody was upset and I thought it would give them something to do.

As for me, I wasn't feeling good. I didn't like the looks of it at all. I pulled Gary aside to get his view. He's young, not long on the force, but he's got a good head and is steady when you need somebody steady.

He said he only got there five minutes ahead of me and hadn't had a chance to look around. His expression was pretty glum. He was as pessimistic about her as I was. I told him to put on a more cheerful face, he wasn't helping matters. Then I said to the others that they should wait there for the dogs to be brought down, and that, meanwhile, Gary and I would search the grounds.

Jim Anders wanted to go with us, but I said I wanted him to keep the others calmed. He was Sally's father and they'd all be looking to him. He wanted to know what I thought could have happened to her, and I couldn't tell him. I said I wanted him to be in charge at the house and look after Mrs. Anders, that I didn't want a lot of people tramping around in case there were any clues.

He didn't want to go back inside. He wanted to be out and around. He wanted to be active. They all do. But he knew I wouldn't let him go with me—in case I found her—and he allowed me to persuade him.

I got a handlamp from the car and Gary and I started over the grounds. The lawn around the house was mowed to the forsythia bushes along the stone wall edging Peach Lane, and down the slope to the south as far as the swimming pool. Below that, a field stretched out for half an acre, buried under lush spring grass. Jimmy Kane mows it for them twice a year for the hay, I understand.

The barn and patio lights lit up the lawn and I couldn't see any signs that meant anything. Down the slope the clumpy grass wasn't deep enough to show tracks, but I led Gary down there anyway. I don't know why. Maybe some of the grass looked bent. Maybe it was instinct.

We crisscrossed the lower field, back and forth, all the way to the end, where a line of undergrowth and parts of a fence bound the wetlands beyond. That's where my lamp caught a spot of white, something different from what was supposed to be there. I knew it was the girl before I went over.

Gary was beside me, off my right shoulder, when we got to her, and he said, "Oh, God."

I don't blame him. It was Sally's body and she'd been battered such as I won't try to describe, except you couldn't tell her hair was blond anymore. It was red with blood. And her face? There wasn't much of it left.

But it was Sally, even if you had to tell more from her shape and her clothes than her face. I knew it, not by the appearance, but by the way of her, and I couldn't help remembering how pretty she'd looked on stage in the first scene of *Oklahoma!* in a window, on a beautiful morning, combing her hair.

Anyway, that's where we found her, face up, about seventy-five yards from the house, her head smashed, maybe with a hammer, and I felt a sick feeling go through me. No matter how many times, when it's a young person, I get that sick feeling.

Her blouse had been ripped open and her torn bra was up around her neck. She was wearing white cotton socks which were grass- and bloodstained, and one of her shoes was off. It was lying beside her.

She had on a white print skirt that was half up her thighs and I lifted it enough to see that her pants were missing. Beside me, Gary was swearing a blue streak under his breath, trying not to cry.

I put the skirt back the way it was and gripped him by the arm. "Now I'm going to tell you what we do," I said. "We're going back to the car and while I'm radioing headquarters, you're going to go into the house and tell Mr. Anders that I'd like to talk to him. Just Mr. Anders, nobody else. Then you're going to come back here and stand guard over the body. Nobody's to come near. Nobody's to come down off that lawn, you understand? That's your assignment until you're relieved."

Gary nodded. He said, "You going to tell him about his daughter?"

"That's *my* assignment."

"God, I'd hate to have to do that."

"If you hope to rise in the ranks in the police department," I told him, "you're going to have to learn how. It goes with the territory."

Friday May 8

MARTHA HICKEY

I first heard about it at half past two when the phone rang. Because Herb, my husband, is the police chief, we don't usually get calls at night. Even if there's a tractor-trailer crash on the turnpike, or half a dozen teenagers wipe themselves out coming home from a binge, Herbert's not supposed to be bothered. Even if you got a big robbery, like out on Clarkson Road last February. Let the captains take care of it. That's what they're there for. Herbert can be briefed when he gets in in the morning and take charge from there.

So when the phone went off in the middle of the night, and Herb answered and said a couple of very quiet "I sees" and did a lot of listening, I knew this wasn't any wrong number or prank call.

So I'm sitting straight up in bed in the dark when he puts down the phone, and I want to know what's happened. And he won't tell me. All he says is, "I don't know yet, but I'll have to go out. You go back to sleep." And he starts getting dressed.

41

Me go back to sleep? He oughta know better'n that! I kept after him. Most of the time I can worm it outta him. He tries to keep his police work private—claims I can keep a secret like I lay off chocolates. I tell him I only blab to people I can trust. One way or another, though, I get it outta him. But not this time. All he'd say was he didn't know himself what it was all about, which is a lot of horsefeathers. He wasn't taking himself off in the middle of the night without knowing why.

I thought he'd be back in an hour and I'd find out then. So I turned on the lights and made coffee and watched TV. But it was almost half past six and I was dozing in my chair and the TV was all snow before I heard his car in the drive.

He came in and his uniform looked kinda askew, like he hadn't been careful about his looks, which he usually is, because chief of police is an important position in this town and he takes it seriously and wants to set a good example.

But it was his face. He looked ten years older, showing wrinkles I hadn't never noticed before. So I said, "Herbert, sit down. Let me get you some coffee." He eased down at the kitchen table while I pulled my wrap around me because it was real chilly, and I heated up the coffee. "It's bad, ain't it?" I said, not wanting to pressure him. "You going back to bed?"

He shook his head. He'd be going in to headquarters as soon as he shaved and cleaned up. Then he told me about it. I didn't even have to ask. The Anders girl, he told me. She'd been murdered while she was baby-sitting for the Parkers. They'd found her body down in the field below the house.

He said he got there about the time the town ambulance did. Harry Watkins was taking photographs. The Anders were out on the lawn with the Parkers and Whitesides and the woman across the street. They were dazed. They didn't know what hit 'em.

He stayed till the body got put aboard the ambulance. The autopsy, he said, would probably be done at Yale-

New Haven. There were injuries to her head, he said. By
the looks, she might have been beaten with a hammer.
Right then, he said, it was light enough and some of the
men were searching the area for the murder weapon. The
dead girl didn't have any pants on and it was expected
that she'd been raped, but they'd have to wait for the
autopsy report to be sure.

"You got any idea who did it?" I poured him some
coffee and had some myself and got the milk outta the
fridge. All I could think of was, it couldn't happen here.
Not a place like here.

"Yeah," Herb said. "We got a pretty good idea. I got all
the cars out looking for him, but I got a pretty strong
feeling he's at least a hundred miles away by now."

That was when he told me about the stranger. He said
that, after the body'd been taken away, he went back to
headquarters. Detective Harris had already questioned
everybody at the Parkers' and got nothing, and Herb
didn't want the patrol cars wandering aimlessly around,
looking to pick up anybody they found walking on the
roads or driving drunk. He wanted a focus.

Like he said, this wasn't the kind of crime anybody in
town would commit, and he was looking for someone
coming in from outside—reports of thieves coming down
from New Haven to make a strike and beat it back.

There weren't any of those, at least not this night. But
there were those two reports about this strange, insolent
white man who'd shown up at Mrs. Meskill's fence and
later in Millie Stone's backyard. The Parkers' house lies
between the two and, also, the Anders don't live far from
Millie's. The thinking was that the stranger might have
seen Sally in town and might have tracked her. In any
case, he was their one hot lead, their only suspect.

So what Herb did was have a call put in to Millie and
Mrs. Meskill and send a patrolman to each place to question them about the stranger and get as good a description
of the man as they could give. In fact, they're supposed to
come down to the station house this morning and work
with Betty Lumpkin, who's an artist in town, trying to

work up a sketch of what the guy looks like. Once they've
got that, Herb'll talk to Sam Walker, publisher of the
Shoreline News, about printing up flyers for distribution.

Most of the time, when I get gossip about what goes on
in town, especially the kind of stories Herb can tell—
because the juiciest ones get told to the police—I can't
wait to pass them along. I've got a dozen friends like me
and we can fill a morning nonstop swapping tales back and
forth. But when Herb went off to headquarters at half past
seven, the news I had to tell, I didn't want to talk about. I
felt sick all over. I could imagine where that little girl was
right now, lying on a slab in the morgue in Yale-New
Haven Hospital—I've never seen the morgue there but I
could picture it—and I could imagine that pretty soon the
pathologist would be coming in to cut her up. And I could
think about Mr. and Mrs. Anders. I don't know them,
except by sight, maybe to nod to, but they seem like nice
people—never did anybody any harm. And the Parkers!
Can you imagine what it's like to hire a girl to baby-sit and
come home and find she's been murdered in your own
home? God, the *guilt* they must feel. I'd want to *die*!

So I just sat in the kitchen over another cup of coffee,
and then, at one minute after eight, the phone rang, and
it was Emmy Daitch. Emmy's a reporter for the *Shoreline
News* and is a good friend of mine. Herb doesn't like it
that we're chummy, says she's only my friend because I
tell her the police department secrets, but she's loyal and
true and has never yet published anything I've told her
not to. Herb's suspicious and wants to know why I should
tell her things she's not going to publish, and she tells me
that what she knows but can't publish helps her with the
things she can. She says that's why I can trust her. Herb
doesn't, though. He thinks that someday Emmy's going to
come forth with some kind of Peyton Place exposé and
ruin the reputation of everybody in town.

Anyway, it was Emmy, calling right at eight. I'd told
her once, when she was hot after a story and got me out of
bed at seven-thirty (it was Herb's day off), that nobody
with proper manners called before nine in the morning or

after nine at night (some aunt told me so) and that, under
no circumstances—even if there was an earthquake—was
she to call me before eight o'clock. And she remembered
that.

Of course she'd heard about the murder and she wanted
everything I could tell her about it. The *Shoreline News* is
a weekly and wouldn't come out until next Thursday, but
Sally's killing would still be reported in detail and she
wanted all the inside dope to help, as she says, "shape"
her story.

So I gave her what I could. Herb hadn't said any of it
was secret. But Emmy knew more than I did because she'd
been on the phone to headquarters for whatever they'd tell
her, just before she called me. They'd found the murder
weapon, she said. It was down in the field and, like Herb
thought, it *was* a hammer. In fact, Emmy said, it was a
hammer Mrs. Parker had left on the kitchen table. She
was hanging a new clock on the wall and had just finished
when Sally came, and she forgot to put the hammer back.

When Emmy got through, I had another cup of coffee
and decided I wasn't going to get any more sleep than
Herb. I wasn't the least bit sleepy. Too much was happening outside and I needed to be up on things. After all, the
wife of the chief of police ought to know at least as much
as everybody else about what's going on.

The phone started ringing at nine, and I didn't get out
until quarter of ten. I drove in to headquarters; Herb was
closeted with Mr. Parker and the other police commissioners in a special meeting. There was a TV truck and
crew from New Haven with guys by the desk with mikes
and cameras and miles of cable, waiting to get something
on tape for the evening news.

I asked Leo—Sergeant Winch—what was new, and he
looked uncomfortable, what with the newsmen leaning
closer. "Nothing much."

"They found the hammer. Where?"

"Uh—in the field. Near the edge of the property." He
gave a glance to the TV people. "We haven't identified it
yet as the murder weapon."

"Thrown from where the body was found?" (I haven't been a policeman's wife twenty-eight years for nothing.)

"Uh, possibly."

"The body. Was she killed where she was found?"

"Uh, I think you ought to ask your husband."

"I'm asking *you*."

"Uh, we think maybe."

As I say, I haven't been a policeman's wife twenty-eight years for nothing. But Leo was sweating and I let him go.

Then the TV people wanted to ask me questions. I told them I didn't know anything—if I did, why would *I* be asking questions? Like I say, I'll tell Emmy anything, because I can trust her. But those bastard media people from out of town, they'd spill my guts if they could get to 'em.

I went out to the supermarket. That's where to find the housewives on a Friday morning. And I'm one of 'em. That's where to get the gossip.

You got it right, the noise level was ten decibels higher and all the talk was about the murder. You could feel the shock waves bouncing off the walls. Everyone was shook up. I mean, they're mostly women in there, and women know how vulnerable they are—especially to something like this. It panics us. Deep down, it scares us like nothing you can believe!

And they were mad. The ones who knew me, they didn't say it, but you could hear it from the others. "How come the police didn't do anything?" The word had spread. There'd been a stranger in town. The way the talk was going, he'd shown up all over the place. He'd tried to steal a bicycle from a yard on Fair Street. He was chased out of a parked car on Bishop Street. The way the rumor factory was working, he'd already been seen and chased a half-dozen times. By midafternoon, you could bet the rumored sightings would be an even dozen.

And, of course, all the sightings were made by civilians. The police hadn't been anywhere around. Complaints had been phoned in to headquarters—four or five, according to what one woman was saying. "And the cops ignored them." That's what she said.

"I heard they were out looking, but couldn't find him," her companion said.

"Just like 'em," the first one answered. "Everybody in town sees him except the cops."

Well, I didn't blame 'em for bitching. They were scared. But I didn't like it that they were taking it out on the cops. The cops paid attention to those two reports. They were out looking for that stranger. But Mrs. Meskill didn't call in her complaint until a couple of hours after it happened, and there's no telling where a guy can get to in two hours. That's the trouble with most people. Millie Stone was better. She was pretty prompt. Not prompt enough. She didn't run right to her phone. And the descriptions weren't any good. The men in the patrol cars could only look for somebody they didn't know by sight, who looked as if he didn't belong. And if he didn't want to be spotted, he wouldn't have any trouble keeping out of their way.

Hell, even if he *got* spotted, he hadn't done anything. Herb's men couldn't do more than ask him what he was doing in town, what he wanted. And if they didn't like his answers, all they could do was take him to the edge of town and tell him to be on his way. Those women, Millie and Mrs. Meskill, they weren't about to swear out a complaint or anything.

That's the trouble. The cops can't arrest a person until *after* he's committed a crime. But that's not their fault.

But they were sure getting the blame for what happened to Sally, there in the supermarket.

Herb came home for lunch at half past twelve and he was having a bad time. First there'd been that meeting with the police commissioners. Mr. Parker was real upset. They all were, but Sally'd been baby-sitting for him and he'd seen the body. He's a commissioner, and you couldn't stop him from seeing the body if he wanted to.

So there they'd been, in the meeting room, putting their heads together with Herb, wanting to know what was being done to track down that stranger. Herb told them there was an eight-state alarm out and that Millie and Mrs. Meskill were coming in to work with Betty Lumpkin drawing up a picture. And, of course the grounds were being searched. And the hammer, of course, was checked and, of course, there weren't any fingerprints. And Herb's men were going door to door in the area where the stranger'd been reported to see if anybody besides Mrs. Meskill and Millie Stone had seen him.

The commissioners had some kooky ideas of their own, of course, like checking all truck stops along I-95 in case the stranger had fled to the turnpike and thumbed a ride with some trucker who made a pit stop along the way and the stranger might have bought a sandwich. Or dust the whole Parker house for fingerprints. Mr. Parker didn't like that idea any more than Herb did—getting that powder over everything for nothing. Those commissioners read too many mystery stories. They think you leave fingerprints on everything you touch.

So Herb had to deal with them and not let them tie up his men on too many wild-goose chases. Then there was a problem with getting a picture drawn of what the stranger looked like. First, Mrs. Meskill and Millie Stone had only the vaguest recollection, and second, they couldn't agree. They couldn't even agree on the clothes he was wearing, except he had on a plaid shirt with a torn sleeve.

And, of course, there were the phone calls. Everybody in town was calling in wanting to know what was being done, wanting to give advice, wanting to complain how such a terrible thing could be allowed to happen in our town, and make the pointed suggestion that the whole police force needed an overhauling.

Herb didn't say anything over lunch, but I think it was gnawing at him underneath that if he couldn't catch that stranger it could mean his job.

Friday and Saturday, May 8–9

EMILY DAITCH

Friday's supposed to be a day off for reporters for the *Shoreline News* except, of course, when some big story breaks. Like the Sally Anders case.

How I first heard about it was over the Plectron box, which is tied in to all the fire department calls and ambulance emergencies. It's not mine. I don't want to know what goes on, to tell the truth. A weekly newspaper isn't like a daily. It doesn't deal with scoops and being first on the street with the scandals in town. Most of the scandals in town never get revealed. I know, because I know them all. Well, I pride myself I know most of them. Most people tell me things. Because they know I won't print what's secret. I could write a book, though, if I really wanted to blow the whistle. Like Truman Capote. You can do it—but only once. After that, you're a corpse. Like Truman. Nobody will ever speak to you again.

So I'm not writing any exposés of the people in this town while I'm a reporter for the *Shoreline News*. And, let's face it—I'm ashamed to say—I never will. I know

these people too well. I like them. And they know me too
well too. They know I'd *never* tell. If they didn't know
that, they wouldn't tell me the things they do. And if you
think I'm going to mention here, in this statement, any
names or any scandals around town that aren't already
known, you'd better forget it. This is *my* town. I live here.
I know this place like nobody else, because nobody else
can prowl and hunt and question and get answers better
than I can.

To get back to Thursday night, the Plectron box belongs
to my husband, Bill. Bill likes being connected to the fire
and emergency calls. He's in the CVFD—Crockford Volunteer Fire Department to you city slickers—and he got
eligible for a Plectron and, believe me, he got one. Bill's
as interested in what goes on in town as I am, except that
he wants to know the man things, if you know what I
mean. He wants to be up on all the fires and accidents,
wherever they are—all the horrible things that go on
(and you'd better believe it), *even* in a small town like
ours.

I don't care about that. I want to know about *people*. I
want to know their problems, how they feel, how they
cope. Bill's a sexist. He says mine is women's work. He
says I want to know the inside of people's guts; and only
women care about that. He's a *male*. He says I'm never to
forget that. (Believe me, I don't.) He says "mayhem and
crisis" is what life's about.

And let me tell you, he can deal with crisis! He owns a
liquor store. (That may not sound like much, but Bill's is
the liquor store in town.) And he's been held up twice—by
dope addicts out of New Haven (I can give you better
names for them, but I won't). And none of them got away
with a cent. Bill keeps a gun under the counter. One will
never walk again; the other's in jail for a long time (which,
today, means, like, eighteen months). I worry about Bill,
but he laughs.

But, no getting around it, he *deals* with a crisis.

Like at fires! God, he's a maniac, fighting fires. You'd
think he was fighting Satan for sure. He's not going to live

long, I can tell you that—You're going to die, Billy my
love. Too young, too soon.

He's forty-four. It's longer than I ever expected. The
dumb, stupid clod, he's always asking to be killed. Like
the time, getting the kid out of the burning house. She
was two years old, and her nightgown was on fire. And he
brought her out. And his hair was scorched off his head.

I'm talking nonsense. You don't want to hear about Bill,
or me, or about Bill Jr., who does volunteer ambulance
duty.

What happened—and now I'm trying to tell it straight—is
Bill Jr., our son, twenty-four years old, unmarried, still
living at home, sleeping in our cellar—we fixed it up for
him—got the emergency call.

All right, he and Eddie Wald, who's the paramedic with
him, were aboard the ambulance behind the town hall in
like no time you'd believe. Eddie and we both live on
Grove Street, and we've timed it to the ambulance—from
both homes—in 3:48. That was the record. Billy says he
was behind the wheel, turning on the ignition, with Eddie
into the seat beside him—and rolling, in 3 minutes 45
seconds! Even when Lance Bell, who pioneered the local
ambulance system, went for broke, he couldn't get from
Gong to Ignition in less than 3:41.

Not that it mattered this time. What they drove to
Yale-New Haven Hospital in the back of the town ambulance was not an emergency case, but the body of a cute
little blond high school junior. And it wasn't with sirens
and lights. Sally Anders was dead and they drove real
quiet. And it wasn't to the ER for salvation; it was to the
morgue for autopsy—to find out what had happened to
her and what had been done to her.

My Bill was up the moment the Plectron sounded.
Most reports are unimportant and they all sound alike. An
emergency sounds different. Bill can sleep all night through
the usual, brush fire stuff, even though the Plectron's on

his side of the bed. But let an emergency sound, and he's like the fire horses of old. He's up and champing.

That's how I knew something was going on. I can't sleep through him jumping up. Maybe there's some of it in me too. He ran out and I could hear him and Bill Jr. downstairs as Billy went out the door.

After that, there was no more sleep for Bill. He sat on the edge of the bed and smoked cigarettes, listening to the reports. I sacked out, leaving it for Bill to tell me what it was about and whether I should get up and go some-place. I guess I'm not an ace reporter, but I'm not into emergencies like Bill and Billy. They don't affect me the same way.

So I didn't really get the details until half past four, when Billy and Eddie got back from the hospital. I could hear them in the kitchen, over coffee with my Bill, talk-ing. I went down and had coffee with them and they went back to bed, but not me. Not after what they said.

And what I had to do was kill time till I could call Martha. You know, Herb's wife—the chief of police. That wasn't till eight. Martha gets cranky if you call before eight. You'd think the wife of the chief of police would be used to getting calls at all hours. But you have to go carefully with Martha. She's not somebody you want mad at you when you're a reporter for the *Shoreline News*, especially since she doesn't get any kick out of seeing her name in the paper. She doesn't want to compete with Herb. Besides, she knows how you get your head chopped off if you get too prominent. Any wife of anybody in public office feels the slings and arrows, even if they're only directed at their husbands. They feel them worse than their husbands.

If I was reporting this story properly, like for the *Shore-line News*, I wouldn't be giving all this sideline stuff. I'd be paraphrasing for you what I've written for the next issue of the paper, due on the fourteenth.

But today's only the eighth and most of what I'll tell you won't get into the paper. Like the autopsy.

All right, it's Friday morning. I call the police at ten of
eight, because I can't stand it another minute not getting
any news. I don't like calling the police, if you really want
to know. They make me feel uncomfortable. They're so
standoffish, so damned chary about giving out information. Maybe it's because I'm a woman. But at least they
do tell me about the hammer. Next, I phone Martha
Hickey to get everything she knows. After that, I do what
she does that morning—I circulate and ask questions. I
know about the mysterious stranger and that our newspaper
will publish—*free* (and that says something for Sam Walker,
the publisher, who'll sell you his soul if the price is
right)—flyers printing the murderer's picture and description for circulation all over the eastern states.

The only trouble is, the police don't know *who* he is or
where he is.

I know Martha, and I do deal with the police a lot, and
I think I understand them. So I empathize with the spot
they're in: The lovely young daughter of one of the *best*
families (if that sounds snide, you don't understand this
town) was beaten and murdered while baby-sitting for a
family friend's children. The question on the lips of everyone in this community is: "How could such a thing happen in this lovely town?"

The *how* was obvious. Ever since, in the mid-fifties, the
I-95, the Connecticut Turnpike, sweeping from the borders
of New York to the boundary of Rhode Island, has provided
not only an easy exurban location for Yale professors who
wanted to live out of town, but a thruway route for trucks,
caravans, and itinerants, some of whom might suspect that
our town was the honeycomb in the beehive.

The *who* was something else again!

Herb was doing his best, getting Dorothy Meskill and
Millie Stone to provide a description of the "stranger."
But if he knew anything about women, he'd know it
wouldn't work.

Before now, Dorothy and Millie hardly spoke to each
other. Three years ago, they'd both served on the Nurse's

Association for a term. There'd been some differences of opinion and when Dorothy replaced Millicent as head, Millie had *withdrawn*.

Now, however, each was vitally aware of the other, and nothing lay quiet.

The two of them eventually drew what, in reluctant concert, represented the features of the stranger whom both had encountered at their garden gates, and who had invaded their privacy in an unseemly way. They did reach reasonable agreement as to his clothes—at least to a plaid shirt with a tear in the right sleeve. What else he wore, and the structure of his face, they quarreled about.

This flyer was put on the presses Friday afternoon and, by the close of the workday, was baled and ready for distribution to newspapers, police stations, post offices, and a select coterie of "bars" all over New England, New York City, upper New Jersey and eastern Pennsylvania. "That should bring him to earth pretty fast," Herbert assured a special meeting of outraged, frightened citizens at the high school at seven o'clock that evening. Police commissioners Don Harding and Hugh McCormick sat on the stage behind him, somber as slate, nodding soberly, wanting everybody to believe what Herb said.

Except police commissioner Charlie Parker was missing. His home had been the scene of the crime and he wasn't there. Maybe he couldn't show his face. Maybe he was grieving. Maybe a lot of things.

He wasn't at the Anders' though. Neither was Pam Parker. I know that for a fact. The Anders' relatives had come in from all over, and their neighbors. They brought in food—enough to feed an army—and comfort; the warmth of comfort eases pain a little. And support. When you get hit like that, though, you live in shock. You don't feel pain or grief, only numbness and disbelief. It's only after the relatives and friends, neighbors and supporters go away that the numbness goes away too, and the reality hits you that Sally isn't ever going to come home again. That's the time when you really need the comfort and the help.

It looked like everybody who wasn't at the Anders', helping how they could, was at the high school listening to the police chief, hoping he could still their fears.

I apologize if I sound bitter, but I'm a bitch on wheels. I stood and watched and listened, and those concerned citizens filling two thirds of the high-school auditorium weren't making the trip because they cared about Sally Anders. Half of them never heard of her. They were worrying about themselves. "If it can happen to *her*, how safe am I?" That's what they were thinking. And I can tell you that for sure, because three quarters of that audience was women.

But the Parkers weren't at either place. And they weren't at home, either. Or if they were, they didn't have any lights on and they didn't answer the door or the phone. I think they were in hiding. I should've checked, but I don't think either of them—or their kids—were in town.

Tracking Sally's murderer to earth was not, to me, the crux of the matter. What, to me, was important, was what had been *done* to her. I'm not trying to present myself as a feminist, per se, nor as a traditionalist.

But—

To put it frankly, *I abhor rapists.*

In pursuit of my particular concern—the wanton rape of women—I attended the autopsy on Sally's body. Never mind my credentials, or the strings I pulled. Never mind the autopsy itself. I've been to them before, and a description, other than to assure the reader that it is through a viewer's eye, is irrelevant. Most people get squeamish at the thought of cutting open human bodies and examining what's inside. So let's skip through to the results.

What the autopsy showed—and I was a witness myself— was that Sally Anders had both been raped and beaten to death, in that order.

And the murder weapon was the hammer found in the bushes.

Saturday May 9

PEGGY BODINE
It's not all that surprising, y'know what I mean? People
your own age dying. Even people you know. Like, you
take my folks. Somebody in their class in high school in
New Haven, like where they grew up, got killed in a car
accident one New Year's Eve. A girl. It was a big deal
back then, y'know what I mean? Because back in those
days, nobody <u>young</u> ever died. I mean, almost never!
That's why it was such a big deal, this girl, on New Year's
Eve, and the roads were slippery. And you wanna know
the climax? They didn't even <u>know</u> the girl. The closest
they got was they had a study hall in the girl's home
room.
And my folks would shake their heads about how they'd
been brushed by death.
Hell, it's nothing nowadays. And it's not just in the
newspapers, y'know what I mean? It happens all the time.
And I don't just mean the <u>first</u> time it ever happened,
which was in third grade and Bobby Darrow died of spinal
meningitis. Hell, he sat behind me in Miss Rutledge's

home room. He used to draw pictures on his pads when Miss Rutledge was talking. Pictures of sheep, mostly. I guess they were sheep. They looked like sheep to me, y'know what I mean? I kinda admired him. He kinda awed me. I couldn't draw a straight line. And he would sneak me glances at the things he was drawing, and we had to make sure Miss Rutledge wasn't looking, and we'd snicker together. I don't mean I was in love with him or had a crush on him, or anything like that, y'know what I mean? We just kinda had fun together because we sat so close. And what else are you gonna do in school when someone like Miss Rutledge is teaching you things?

He used to tell me he was going to be an artist when he grew up. He could draw Snoopy real good. He was going to do a comic strip about a lamb. But, like I say, he got spinal meningitis and he wasn't in school anymore. Not that we knew what was wrong with him, y'know, only that he was sick. We didn't even know when he died. And the teacher put Ralph Mazzorati behind me, in Bobby's seat. But Ralph was a stupe, y'know what I mean? Who'd want to turn around in her seat to talk to <u>Ralph</u>?

So death isn't a big deal, y'know what I mean? Hell, there's been at least one teenager killed in a car crash every single year since I got to high school. And most of them I knew—at least by sight. Y'know what I mean? You get <u>used</u> to people you know dying—and I don't just mean great-grandparents and people like that who're a hundred and thirty years old. I mean fifteen, sixteen, seventeen— especially seventeen. You hear about the crash last year? Two guys and two girls, seventeen, and the only survivor was a fourteen-year-old brother who was <u>driving</u> the car? And he's paralyzed from the neck down.

So, y'know what I mean, we <u>live</u> with death. And I'm not even talking about the three high-school suicides over the past year, which aren't even reported in the paper— but the adults can't hide it from us kids, for all their secrecy. We know more about why they did it than their parents do. Hell, their parents don't know a goddam thing. Parents <u>never</u> do. That's why the kids do it—well, it's one of the reasons, anyway.

But listen to me talk. My teachers would love that! They can't get me to open my mouth.

But that's not what I'm talking about, y'know what I mean? I'm talking about what happened to Sally Anders and the viewing the funeral parlor had for her Saturday evening. I think Catholics call it a "wake." I don't really know what Protestants say it is, even though I'm one, and I've said good-bye to a lot of my friends this way.

Like the others—y'know—the ones who got killed in car crashes, and there've been a couple of ODs in our school as well (but nobody's supposed to know that, especially us kids). Except, of course, we <u>all</u> do. It's only our parents who don't know what the hell's going on, and pretend they do, and shut their mouths the moment their children enter the room. They think they're the ones doing the <u>hiding</u>.

But Sally was different.

The way <u>she</u> died—I mean—you come to expect certain things. You know about drugs and drink and driving, and that we kids are gonna do it all—including sex. I don't mean to leave out sex. But we're only starting to include sex now because of AIDS. Pregnancy hasn't been all that big a deal. Mostly it doesn't happen. I mean, to anybody who's got <u>any</u> intelligence!

But Sally didn't die like anybody else in this town! She was my best friend and I'd've mourned her no matter <u>how</u> she died. But any other way wouldn't have been so much a surprise—I mean, even if it turned out she OD'd on drugs. It's done in our school, y'know what I mean? There're those "elements" in the school who go in for that sort of thing. But Sally wasn't in it, any more than I am. I'd've sworn to it.

Even so, y'know, I'd've been <u>less</u> surprised if I heard she'd OD'd, than to hear she'd been <u>murdered</u>!

I mean <u>MURDERED</u>? And raped? Well, if she's gonna be murdered, what could you expect? Why else would

anybody murder a nice kid like Sally except because she
was a girl. Lust, lust, lust! That's what it was, and I'm
gonna cry. It wasn't her fault she was a girl.

But that's the terrible part, y'know what I mean? That
she was murdered for sex. They oughta castrate the bastard. That's what I'd do!
Anyway, you wanta hear about the "viewing," or whatever church people call it. I mean, I go to church. Hell,
Sally and I sing in the choir—well, I won't be singing in it
anymore. Sally won't and neither will I. But we were only
in it for the singing. We didn't pay attention to the service. I never will understand what religion's all about.

All right, I keep forgetting. It's my nature, y'know what I
mean? You want to hear about the viewing. Well, it was
Saturday night. Seven to nine. I got there early, quarter
to seven—me and Fritzie and Laura and Pat. We came in
Fritzie's car and had a couple of snorts before we went in.
I mean, that kind of stuff is heavy, man. Not enough to
get giggly, but enough so we could handle all the old folks
and their forlorn faces. I mean, we kids—we knew her.
She was us. We can miss her our own way, and never
mind the long faces of all the grown-ups. They never
knew her. Even her parents never knew her. We were
the only ones who could really commune with her. But
not at a viewing, not in front of all the adults. This was
their show and we'd play it their way—look solemn, say a
prayer or bow or do something at the coffin, and take a
seat near the back of the room and watch who came and
who did what.
There were flowers all around. Mr. Salmon, who's head
of the Salmon Funeral Home, our biggest, let us in, even
though we were early. Mr. and Mrs. Anders and Christopher were sitting in the front row of seats before the
mahogany coffin, and all you could smell in the dim room
were flowers. Lights shone on the coffin, so that was
bright, but the rest of the room was dim. And, thank God,
the coffin was closed. Y'know what I mean? I don't think I

coulda stood it seeing Sally dead. Especially what we heard about her being beaten with a hammer. I've been to funerals before and I've seen dead bodies, and the funeral people fix them up real pretty and try to make them look almost like they were sleeping. But Miss Rainer, who died of cancer and who was maid to my mother, didn't look like Miss Rainer, she looked like a skeleton, she was so withered and gaunt and gray. Until then, I always thought of her as giddy and plump and red-faced, and always laughing. Now I don't like to think about her anymore.

Frankly, I was scared, going into that room. I mean, there was Mr. and Mrs. Anders and Chris. And, God, I was terrified, y'know what I mean? What do you <u>say</u>? I mean, <u>what</u> <u>do</u> <u>you</u> <u>SAY</u>? That's why we went together, Fritz, Laura, Pat and me. I couldn't have <u>gone</u> there by myself, especially if the coffin was open. If I'd've had to see Sally's face, I would've died. Because I knew it wasn't her face anymore, it'd been fixed up by the funeral parlor people to try to <u>look</u> like Sally's face, and I could tell. For all the years we'd known each other, grown up together, and laughed and sang, and talked, and sometimes we even cried (not more than once or twice, and that's none of your business), there's no way they could have patched up her head and made me believe it was Sally.

It was in the right front room. The windows beyond the coffin faced on Church Street, but they were closed off by curtains. In front of them was the beautiful mahogany coffin. The Anders must really be rich. You never saw such a beautiful coffin! And flowers! Like I say, they were everywhere! It kinda made me think—and I'm ashamed to say this—that I'd like it the same way when I die. You know what I mean? You couldn't die <u>better</u>. If you <u>have</u> to die, that is.

And there were all those flowers. Baskets of roses flanking the coffin. White flowers in other baskets. There was a spray of lilies on top of the coffin. I can tell you about roses and lilies. I don't know many other flowers.

And there was the smell of them. And that beautiful

coffin with the spray of lilies on the top, and white crepe
streamers, and, thank God, the coffin was closed. All I
could think was, "How do we <u>really</u> know Sally's body's
inside? Who knows but they could bury that coffin tomorrow, and Sally wouldn't be there at all!"

But I shouldn't be admitting to such thoughts, y'know
what I mean? It doesn't make me sound like a good friend
to Sally. But that's not true. Sally and I were <u>real</u> friends.
It was only this—this formal stuff that didn't seem real.
Even seeing Mr. and Mrs. Anders and Christopher sitting
so quiet and solemn in front of that sleek, elegant coffin
didn't make it seem <u>real</u>.

We—Fritz, Laura, Pat and me—went in a line past the
coffin. Mr. Salmon directed us, but I didn't have to be
shown, y'know what I mean? I'd done it before. Too many
times. Like Fritz, Laura and Pat. We've done this too
many times, for too many friends. All that made it different
this time was, Sally hadn't done anything to offend the
gods, y'know what I mean? She didn't deserve it.

We bowed over the coffin, the four of us, but I knew
the Anders were watching and I had to bow a little more
and put my forehead down against the wood of the coffin
so they'd know I cared. It didn't mean anything. Sally was
no more inside that coffin—even if her body was—than <u>I</u>
was. She was in some foreign world, one I won't know
about until I die too. That's my belief, and I can't tell you
how I came by it. But when I put my forehead down
against the cool polished wood of her coffin, I whispered,
"I'll see you again, Sally. Through all eternity."

All right, you can laugh, but that's exactly what I said.

And then I raised my head and went alone to hold
hands and do—I don't even know what I did—things with
Christopher and Mr. and Mrs. Anders. Somehow, Fritz,
Pat and Laura weren't beside me when I needed them,
and I had to go through this trauma without any help.

I don't know how I did it. Tears were streaming down
Mr. Anders' face. He was holding my hands and telling
me—I don't <u>know</u> what he was telling me—all I remember were those tears. And I didn't know men cried.

Then we were in the back of the room. I don't know
how we got there. All I know is that Fritz, Laura, Pat and
I were through the agony and could take seats as far back
as they had in the room.

And then, promptly at seven o'clock, the mourners
began to arrive. The Anders, they stayed where they
were, and the mourners would come in in a line from the
door, make their obeisance to the coffin, and turn to the
Anders to say whatever it is that people say to the people
who grieve.

To tell you the truth, I wanted to get out of there as
soon as we'd paid our respects. Y'know. It's time to go,
and you <u>go</u>.

But I didn't know, this being my first "murder" case,
exactly how I should behave. So we stayed.

And the people came—and came—and came.

I mean, once the hour for grieving struck, there was no
letup in the number of grievers. I could watch the line
grow, from beyond the room into the vestibule and out
into the street. And always <u>longer</u>. God, I couldn't help
wondering how many people would be showing up if <u>I</u>
was the one who'd died!

You know how teenagers are? If I sound irreverent,
chastise me as you will, but remember, always remember,
in today's society, the teenager has an <u>out</u>! Suicide. I don't
know where I would go or what would happen to me if I
took my own life, but if this life gets too bad, <u>anything</u>
will be an improvement.

Of course, Sally hadn't taken her own life. The <u>Society</u>
had taken it from her.

And what was the Society going to <u>do</u> about it?

That's what I was listening to hear, and <u>I</u> <u>heard</u>. I
mean, we may have sat at the back of the room, but old
people took seats in front of us, and around us, and old
fogies, y'know what I mean, they think teenagers are a
part of the wallpaper. They don't think us teenagers can
think, see, hear, feel, or care.

And you know what the talk was about? Not a word about Sally. Not a word of pity or regret, or caring for what Mr. and Mrs. Anders—and Chris—might be feeling, sitting up at the front of the room, accepting the grievances of all the dozens and dozens of mourners who piled through, not one word of concern for their loss. All those big-wig adults, who're supposed to be role models for us teenagers, talked about, was the abysmal police department this town was supporting, how our police department, Herb Hickey in particular, could have let a killer come into our town, murder a nice kid like Sally Anders, and escape. When I call her "nice kid," you know, I'm talking about how we classmates felt about her. Listening to the grown-ups in the funeral parlor talk about how Herb Hickey should be run out of town on a rail, I could tell "Sally Anders" was just a name to them.

But I have to tell you, it scared me to listen.

Maybe those big-shot adults didn't know Sally, but they were a powerful bunch. When people like them put their heads together, and that's what they were doing, you can better watch out.

I mean, they were mumbling, "Lynching's too good for the likes of him," and that scared the bejesus outta me. I mean, I loved Sally like a sister. I don't really know how I'm gonna get along without her. But we don't really know what happened to her, and when I heard mumblings like that in the row ahead of us, all I could think of was a picture of our proud and beautiful Green in the center of town, and a crowd gathered, and some guy on a platform with a rope around his neck, and everybody cheering because they said he'd raped and murdered Sally Anders and he was going to be hung.

Saturday and Sunday, May 9–10

CHIEF HERBERT HICKEY

It was getting ugly in town Saturday night. They had a vigil on the Green after the viewing. A candlelight vigil—so they called it. All the people who came over from the funeral home. Somebody'd passed the word while they were sitting staring at the coffin. Bert Richards most likely. He likes to stir things up, then sit back and watch what happens. He's on the Board of Finance and you ought to see the monkey wrenches he throws when the police budget comes up. "New police cars? The olds ones only got 120,000 miles on 'em. Have you checked the cost of repairs against the cost of new cars, Chief? I want to see a breakdown." Then he'll sit back and hope the others will take up the cry and make the commissioners and me go back to the drawing board and start over.

His son got arrested for drunk driving six years ago, lost his license for a year, and Bert's had it in for us ever since. In fact, he's tried to get on the police commission, but, thank God, the Republicans turned him down last time and he's got two more years on the Board of Finance. But that's not to say he only baits the police department. He's like that with every department come budget time, but you can tell he especially hates the police force.

So when the mourners marched down Church Street from the funeral parlor to the Green, and lighted candles in remembrance of Sally, you might think it was the vigil it was claimed to be. Especially when candles started being passed around. Mr. Wallace, minister at St. Bartholomew's Church, got them from the parish-house storeroom.

That made it look like a religious thing—even when the group moved from the far end of the Green by the Crockford Congregational Church over to St. Bartholomew's Church. But then the group settled at the corner of Hartford and Green Street, opposite the bank, not the church, and just around the corner from the police station.

That's so we could hear 'em when they started chanting. At first it was just one voice piping up, "We want vengeance, we want vengeance." Then there was some haranguing about what had been done and more voices took up the cry. And pretty soon more people came from around town to join in. You know how the word spreads. "Something's going on at the Green," and people start hurrying on foot or jumping into cars to come see.

I was home when all this started, but at quarter of ten, when over a hundred people were gathered and the chanting was getting loud, Sergeant Winch called me. He was getting nervous that there might be trouble. So I hopped right down and made it a point to drive by the Green, see how big the group was, what its temper was. Some recognized the car when I stopped at the corner before turning up Hartford Street, and there was some boos, which grew into a chorus following me to the station parking area. When I went in the front door, someone was shouting, "Burn the police station!"

Winch was at the desk with Pickens on duty. They were the only ones. The windows were open and you could hear, "Burn the police station!" coming through. I said, "Who the hell's *that* loudmouth, Bert Richards?"

Winch shrugged and said he wouldn't be surprised. Pickens was up and walking around. He's one of the new men and he was nervous. There was that kind of eerie quiet all over town, except for the voices. Like the quiet before a thunderstorm. "Sorry to disturb you," Winch said to me, "but I thought you ought to know."

I said that was what I was supposed to be disturbed for and, except for the candles, it didn't look much like a vigil to me.

"They're getting uglier," Winch said. "That one guy's stirring them up."

"Why the hell aren't the ministers stirring them down?"

"Think I should call in some of the men? Just in case things get out of hand?"

"The hell with that," I said. "They aren't coming here, I'm going there!"

And I took my butt right over to the Green as fast as I could walk, and I was steaming.

Well, the moment I got to the corner where the bank was, and crossed the street to where the crowd was, there was this big chorus of boos, and cries of "There's the bastard," and shrieks of "Why aren't you doing something?" and "What's the matter with the police?" and cries like "This town isn't safe anymore!" and they came inching closer.

It was unnerving. I mean, I know these people—most by name, all by sight. They're supposed to be friends of mine, friendly people, full of goodwill, wishing no one harm; but I had this feeling that they weren't my friends anymore, that they'd lost their sympathy and understanding. They had the look and feel of a mob about them, and a mob, let me tell you, is something to be real scared of. I only encountered a mob once, many years ago, before I ever became a cop, and, let me tell you, I'll never forget it.

That's neither here nor there. The thing is, I marched through the crowd, looking neither right nor left, not answering anything anybody said, making them break ground before me, until I located Walter Wallace, the minister at St. Bartholomew's Church. He was standing, holding a candle, with his finger up his— Well, you know what I mean—not doing anything. And I lit into him. I said, and I mean loud enough so anybody could hear, "What the hell are you doing, standing around doing nothing, letting a lot of people go crazy? Why the hell aren't you telling them to shut up and simmer down? Where the hell's that Prince of Peace you're always talking about? You're supposed to be a goddam leader in this town. *Be* a leader! Tell these people to break up and go home!"

He stared at me kind of stupefied. He'd never been in this kind of quandary before. All he'd ever done was address a congregation and visit the homes of the sick. Always everybody looked up to him and listened. Because he was on his home turf. Maybe that's what it's all about, being a minister. You're always on your home turf. The others are strangers to your territory and they approach with awe and insecurity and a desire to please the head honcho. And they tell themselves how great it is, even if the sermons are pap, and they'll ooh and ah when the great priest or minister strides forward in his glorious vestments!

I gave up religion long ago, as you can tell, but that's neither here nor there either. The point is, I realized the moment I saw him that Walter was frightened. This wasn't his home turf. He'd probably tried to raise his voice and his candle once or twice to seek attention, but he wasn't in church, he was on the Green, and he was being upstaged, and he'd never been in such a spot before, and he didn't know what to do. So, you can't blame him. Put a guy in a strange situation, and he can only go with what he has. And, I'm sorry to say, I don't think Walter Wallace, nice guy that he is, fifteen years priest at St. Bartholomew's Church, knew how to handle a situation that was getting out of hand. He was, deep down inside, a frightened person. If people didn't genuflect when he raised a finger, he didn't know what to do.

The moment I said it, I was sorry I'd berated him. He

tried the beatific smile that's supposed to soothe all, but it was the only answer he had. He turned, raising his candle to silence the stirring crowd, ready to exhort the assembly to disperse.

But the anger was raging inward from the edges of the crowd, from beyond where the vigilantes could hear him or cared to listen, and his raised candle was as fruitless as a match in a hurricane.

At least he was at my side, and that helped. "What are you doing here?" I yelled at everybody. "You can't bring her back! Go home! The police will find the man! I promise you! The police will find the man!"

"How come you let him kill her?" came a voice from the rear. It was Bert Richard's. I know his voice well. And it came from his usual spot—the rear.

"Shut up, Bert," I yelled back. "You want more police protection? You give us the money and we'll give you all you want!"

It was the only thing I could think of, but it was the right response. It directed hostility away from the police, and people's heads turned toward the speaker at the fringe. We didn't hear from him again, and after I once more yelled to the group to disband, bigod, the people began to break up and go away.

At the end, there was only Walter Wallace and me. "You didn't have to do that," he said to me. "Humiliate me in front of my own flock. I was soothing them, holding them down, making them see the error of their ways. They were coming to their senses. I was making it happen."

I wanted to put a hand on his arm—let him know I understood. But I didn't touch him. I'm a lapsed Catholic and I don't know much about religion, but I had the feeling you don't get that familiar with a priest. "I'm sorry," I apologized. "I didn't know the situation was under control. If I had, I wouldn't have spoken."

I don't know if he accepted my apology. I don't know how much my fierce address to the crowd affected his reputation. All I know is, the bomb was defused. There was no march on the police station, no brutality, no damage done to the public buildings by people who'd feel shamed for life in their own eyes had such a thing happened.

Nevertheless, the temper of the town was short. There wasn't a church on Sunday where the priest, pastor, minister—what-have-you, didn't preach a sermon on Sally Anders' murder. They ran the gamut from "Lock your doors" to "Tear up the turnpike via which evil alien elements can infiltrate our precious, special town."

The police commissioners, including Charlie Parker, met with me at headquarters at noon on Sunday, in the hour between the ending of church services and the funeral service for Sally.

They wanted the latest on the search for Sally's killer and I had to confess there was nothing. We went around and around again on what might be done that we weren't doing, and some talk about Bert Richards and his vendetta against the department. I held my temper and didn't express my opinion of some of the nutty ideas the commission suggested. Fortunately, they're intelligent people, even if they aren't knowledgeable, and they didn't go off the deep end on anything. But they were worried, and so was I. We were looking for a needle in a haystack and the townspeople expected us to find it.

The funeral service was held in St. Bartholomew's Church at one that afternoon, the Reverend Walter Wallace officiating.

The church was packed. Standees were everywhere. Seven hundred people turned out.

Every member of the police department, save one standby, was there, including the supernumeraries. Those were my orders.

It was a sad service. Mr. Wallace talked of eternal life and envisioned Sally as going ahead to prepare a way for the rest of us. He did his best, and it may have soothed the souls of many of those present—giving them to picture lovely, bright and charming Sally putting in a good word for them with the Almighty. Not my soul though. The Almighty's too cruel for my taste. And, I'll bet, for Mr. and Mrs. Anders' taste too, for all their faith. Don't talk to me of religion. I don't know of any religion that can satisfactorily explain the death of a child to the parents of that child.

Martha and I drove home after, not talking much. And then Captain Appleby phoned. He'd just returned to duty and word had come in—from Mystic Point, forty miles up the line. They'd caught the stranger!

Wilfred Greene was his name, twenty-three, arrested trying to steal a bicycle. He matched the description— mainly because of the torn right sleeve on his plaid shirt.

Since he was wanted for murder here, not for stealing a bicycle there, we had preference. That meant bringing him back here to Crockford to face charges. I was down at headquarters in ten minutes and, believe me, we spent a busy afternoon arranging with the Mystic Point and State Police how and when to receive him.

Sunday May 10

CAPTAIN NATHANIEL APPLEBY

I want to tell you, I wanted this case solved fast, and I couldn't wait for us to get our hands on that stranger Mrs. Meskill and Millie Stone had told us about. Now we'd caught the stranger—at least we all thought we'd caught him. The ID relayed from Mystic Point matched the description. The man they had in custody was a vagrant, and the clothing matched, down to that torn right sleeve in a plaid shirt.

We were sure we were bringing in the murderer. And don't think I wouldn't like to see him hung on a tree on the Green, like the effigy some high-school students strung up there right after the funeral service—scampering away when our men drove up. There were a dozen of them and Patrolman Mattock, who pulled down the effigy, recognized at least three of them. But that's not important—their action. I mean, they're kids, and they've been hit hard by someone outside their group—and I don't mean a "stranger," I mean an "adult." You have to understand their thinking. I was in the youth division when I was a

71

patrolman and I had a lot of dealings with the high-school crowd. I'm proud to say they accepted me—as much as teenagers can accept an older man, who's a police officer to boot.

But I listened to them and I understood them some— because their woes weren't all that different from my woes when I was their age. I wasn't into drugs. That was one difference. But I could relate to their feelings—more because I'd had those same feelings than because I was into their world. I was never *into* their world. Each generation has its own comforts and quirks, and we cling to ours— The World According to Our Graduation Class. But their world scares me—not as an adult police captain who's seen more horrors than they've yet dreamed about, but because they've seen so much already.

But teenagers hanging effigies on the Green wasn't what was bothering me when I heard that this white male drifter, name of Wilfred Greene, picked up in Mystic Point on attempted bicycle theft, was being shipped back to our town to stand charge for murder of a young local girl who nobody'd ever heard of before, but who was now being publicized as "America's Small-Town Sweetheart."

What was bothering me was, that effigy was a symptom. The atmosphere in town was mean and getting meaner. Dragging that punk bicycle thief back here as fast as I wanted to see him dragged could cause real problems. There was no telling what might happen. To him and to the town. It could be a real sticky situation.

I gotta hand it to Chief Hickey, the way he handled it. He ordered that nothing be said to anybody, including the press, and he scheduled it to have Greene brought in at seven in the evening, when everybody would be having supper. He was as scared as I about the mob that would surround police headquarters if word leaked out that Sally Anders' killer was being brought into town.

I mean: The hell with effigies! Hang the bastard!

To tell the truth, I'd like to *see* him hung. I've got no sympathy for the bleeding hearts who'll tell you he didn't

mean it and, with proper love and sympathy and understanding, he can be converted into a worthwhile member
of society. Pardon the language, but crap on that. I wanted
to kill the slimy sonuvabitch myself. And I'd be willing to
do it with my bare hands, except for this uniform.

Aye, there's the rub. I'm a cop, and I can't do whatever
I want. And I can't let other people do whatever they
want, either. So I have to send the squad car to the Green
to chase away the high-school kids who're hanging the
stranger in effigy because they cared about Sally Anders
and are outraged and frightened that she was killed, and
they want to see the killer killed. I don't blame them.
When I was in high school, I would've been one of the
ringleaders.

But now I'm a police captain and I'm supposed to
maintain law and order. More than that, I'm to protect
the accused because, as is also high up in my training and
understanding, in this country, a man is "presumed" innocent until he's found guilty. You can't lynch a man. You
can't hang an effigy in a mock lynching. Painful as it may
be, you've got to *prove* a man guilty. Those high-school
kids don't seem to know this yet, and I wonder what
they're being taught!

So, on the chief's orders, and they would have been
mine, we kept it quiet that Wilfred Greene was coming to
town. There'd been that effigy hung, and we didn't want a
real hanging. So we kept mum, except for notifying Millie
Stone and Mrs. Meskill that we'd like them to come to the
police station at eight o'clock and not to say anything to
anybody. Eight o'clock was when we figured Wilfred Greene
would be safe to show.

After the funeral and the effigy hanging, the town more
or less settled down, so far as we could tell. We tried to
too, except there was an electricity in the air around
headquarters you just couldn't miss. A reporter from the
New Haven papers hung around for an hour after cover-
ing the funeral and the effigy story, just chewing the fat

and looking for what more was going on than he was being told, and we had to sit on our hands till he left to keep from showing how they itched. Emily Daitch stopped by for a bit, but we don't worry about her. That reporter from New Haven is sharp and shrewd and ambitious. You have to watch what you say around him. Emily's easy. She fancies herself the Town Crier and you can play upon her good opinion of herself to get the news printed just the way you want it.

That doesn't mean we told her any secrets. We're careful what we let her know. Emily's like any woman. Give her a secret and she'll blab it. She means well, but we weren't telling HER we were bringing in a suspect, even if she couldn't see it in print before Thursday.

Don't ask me how the news gets around. Maybe it's osmosis. . . . That's biology. But about seven o'clock, there were half a dozen people gathered on the Green. Just standing, talking, like they had nothing better to do.

By seven-thirty, there were two hundred. They *knew* our secret! There's no goddam way you can keep a secret in this town! I'm convinced of it. No goddam way at all!

They were quiet. I'll say that for them. There were no candles, there was no Walter Wallace out there, and there were no ropes, no ugly talk, no threats against the police or the "stranger." I didn't hear Bert Richards' voice urging action.

But they were there and waiting.

Wilfred Greene arrived at quarter past seven in an unmarked sedan guarded by three members of the State Police. They did it slickly. No sirens, no flashing lights, no striped and painted police car.

They slipped quietly into our parking lot and brought him through the side door in handcuffs, while the crowd over on the Green stood waiting and growing.

The troopers went away as quietly as they'd come, and we had this lad in with us. He was tall, tousled, unshaven and dirty, with a certain boyish charm to his face that told

me right away he was used to having his way with women.
If you don't know the type, *we* know the type. And too
many women who are now dead, or robbed and de-
stroyed, know his type too. He'll catch them with that
quixotic smile, that wayward lock of hair, his intimate look
that suggests, "I'd like to know you better."

With us, of course, his approach was different. He wanted
to know what he was here for, what we thought he could
have done. A baby's innocence was on his face. He hadn't
been told yet of the charge, and he continued to pretend
he didn't know what it was all about.

The chief and I, Detective Sergeant Harry Dean and
Detective Jack Harris, sat down with him in the chief's
office to take off the handcuffs and talk a bit while Patrolman Norton went to pick up Millie and Mrs. Meskill, and
Patrolman Saville rounded up some men for a lineup.
    Wilfred Greene kept up the bewildered act. He kept
asking why we wanted him, why all this to-do? We didn't
tell him anything, but he didn't tell us anything, either.
We asked where he'd been after he left here, what he'd
done, what he was up to, and he was vague. He didn't
remember ever having been here before. He was hitch-
hiking around, he said, looking for work. He claimed he
was raised in Arkansas, but his accent didn't fit his claim.
The chief keeps a cigarette box on his desk to put people
at their ease, but Wilfred said he didn't smoke, though
you could see the nicotine stains between his fingers and
on his teeth.

The ladies showed up at quarter of eight, and by then,
Wilfred Greene was losing his bravado and his eyes were
darting faster and faster, and he kept glancing at the
windows—the link to the outside world—the way guys do
when the tension gets to them and they begin to fall
apart. Sometimes they'll be so nervous that when you
read them their rights, they don't ask for a lawyer, they
break down and confess and get it off their chests. Who-

ever invented the Catholic Church's confessional knew a
helluva lot about human nature.

Norton knocked and stuck his head in and looked at
me. No sign, no nothing. Greene didn't pick up any
information from that.

I went out, and Norton had the two women out where
Lieutenant Hanlon was monitoring the desk. They had
their antennae out full extension. "Did you catch him?
they asked both at once.

"We don't know what we've got," I said, "but we'd like
to see if you can make an identification."

"There's a crowd on the Green," Millie advised me.
"They say you've caught the killer."

"You talked to them?"

"Damned right. With that crowd gathering and you
wanting me here at eight o'clock, I was gonna find out
what I could. You people wouldn't tell me anything."

"Well, we'll tell you now. What we're going to ask you
to do is look at some people and see if you can tell us who
they are."

Both women started to follow me and I said, "No, one
at a time. First you, Millie, then Mrs. Meskill."

I took Millie into our closetlike viewing room where it's
dark and there's a one-way mirror into the next room, which
is where we do fingerprinting, keep records, that sort of
thing. Saville had five of our auxiliary cops standing there
in work clothes, lined up with Wilfred Greene. Wilfred was
next to the end on the right. I said, "Okay, Millie, look
through the window and tell me if you recognize anybody."

She looked and said, "Ohmigod, ohmigod, it's *him.*"

My heart bounced the way it always does when I know
we've got a "make" on a perpetrator. "Who?"

"That one." She pressed her finger against the glass.
"The fifth on the right."

"Who's he?"

"That's the man who murdered Sally Anders. That one!
The fifth one."

"You mean, he's the stranger you and Mrs. Meskill
drew the picture of?"

"Yes, that's right. The man who murdered Sally Anders."
Some people *do* get the bit in their teeth. "What makes
you so sure he's the stranger you saw?"

"That plaid shirt with the tear in it. I'll never forget that
plaid shirt with the tear!"

I brought her out and whispered to the chief. He turned
her over to Ed Norton who took her back to the chief's
room. He told her he needed a statement, but we needed
to keep her away from Mrs. Meskill.

The chief conferred with Sergeant Dean and me. "That
shirt will kill us," he said.

I said, "Have all the men strip to the waist."

Hickey shook his head. "Have him change shirts with
one of the others."

"Chief, no!" I said. "You've got to get the shirt out of
there entirely!"

Hickey said, "I want the shirt to stay."

"Listen," I pleaded, "if Mrs. Meskill identifies the guy
with the shirt, you'll have blown *everything*. We'll have to
let the sonuvabitch go!"

"We'll have to take that chance."

I felt like shaking him. "But, Chief, we've *got* him. He's
in our hands right this moment! If he walks out of here,
we'll never get him again."

The chief said, "What have we got? A plaid shirt with a
tear. D'you want to hang every vagrant wearing a torn
plaid shirt? It's the *man*, not the shirt, we've got to
identify. This is a murder case, Nat," he reminded me.
"We're talking possible death penalty here—if the townspeople have their way. If the witnesses can't identify the
man and not the clothing, we don't have a suspect. The
clothing can change, the *man* cannot."

I didn't like it but the chief is the chief. I figured,
"What the hell, it's *his* neck." At least that's what I was
trying to figure when I went in and made everybody swap
shirts. Deep down, though, I wanted to kill that young,
self-confident bastard with the wayward eyes and enticing
smile.

I oversaw the changing and went back outside. I gave

Hickey an affirmative nod and he looked green around the gills when I asked Mrs. Meskill to come with me to the viewing room. He knew there were now close to three hundred people on the Green, waiting very quietly, but wanting action and expecting action. The chief himself had promised them action. And it all depended on Mrs. Meskill. I felt like the whole world depended on Mrs. Meskill—my world, at least, the department's world, even the town's. That wasn't the kind of spot I wanted to be in—my fate hanging on someone else, a someone else I only knew by name.

I brought her into the little room and closed the door and it was pitch black. She was quiet, controlled—more controlled than I was, let me tell you—and patient. I fumbled trying to find and unhook the cover over the one-way mirror, and I didn't like being so nervous. I've been a cop too long to be nervous. But I was nervous. Because things were going on in this town, ever since the murder, that I never saw before. I was feeling like a rookie on his first patrol.

I found the catch, opened the cover, and she moved close to look at the six men standing against the farther wall, with feet and inches marked off on the plaster behind them. Wilfred Greene was now third from the left, almost in the middle, wearing a green fatigue shirt. His torn, plaid shirt was on Rufus Riley, the guy in the lineup who matched him most closely.

I cursed myself. I should have orchestrated the shirt-changing, not merely watched it. "You goddam bastard," I muttered to myself, for I'd just sabotaged our own identification. Our fate was really in the lap of the gods.

Dorothy Meskill looked through the one-way window and spoke with the firmness of a person who doesn't stay home all the time keeping house for her husband, but who gets up and out and involves herself with community activities. Dorothy Meskill knew where she stood, knew which end was up.

"There's your man, Captain," she said, pointing. And it wasn't to Rufus Riley, it was to Wilfred Greene!

I could've kissed her. But be cautious in police work. Always be cautious. "You're sure? He's not wearing a plaid shirt with a torn sleeve."

She turned to me, the faintest of light through the window revealing that side of her face. "Listen to me," she said, and no mistake. "When a woman fears she might be raped, it's the *face* of the demon she remembers, the look in his eye, the hair peeking from his nose, the texture of his skin, the color of his eyes and the telltale look of them. You see the way his forehead furrows, the slant of his brows, a mole, a blackhead. I'll forget his shirt," she said, "but I'll never forget his face."

"You'll swear to that in a court of law, on the witness stand?"

"Any time," she whispered. "Day or night."

Sunday May 10

DETECTIVE SERGEANT HARRY DEAN

I broke up the lineup. Wilfred Greene got back into his own shirt, the auxiliaries went their way. Greene was shaking his head, looking to me for help. I don't know why he should look to me, just because I think people can be redeemed. I mean, does it show on my face?

He said, as soon as we were alone, as soon as the last auxiliary cop left the room, "Sir? How bad off am I? What's gonna happen to me?"

That's what bothers me! The auxiliary cops who were in the room with him, who had to stand up beside him on the identification deal, hated his guts. He'd killed an innocent young girl in this town and they wanted him to burn in hell. It showed. It was the atmosphere in the room. You couldn't walk into that room and not feel that only the forces of law and order that had been built into those auxiliaries were keeping them from hanging the bastard, not in effigy, but in person, right there and now.

And, of course, he felt it. You couldn't not feel it.

Now, I don't fancy myself as anything but a normal human being, albeit I'm a cop. Cops, sometimes, have to do things other people don't have to do, things they themselves don't want to have to do. So you've made a commitment, which means that sometimes you have to do things that'll turn your stomach. So you say, *Quit!*

But no job's all good and all bad. In my own quiet way, I have the feeling that the good I do being a cop outweighs the bad I sometimes have to do being a cop. On balance, I think I brighten my corner more than I tarnish it. So I keep on being a cop and rising in the ranks. Because as I rise, I can, maybe, get the police to understand a little better the standpoint of the guilty, get them to be not so ruthless and righteous, and, also, so racist.

By racist, I don't mean here. In this town, we don't have racism. There're blacks here, not many, but a number, and I don't mean just token blacks. Because they range the gamut. One's a garbage collector, another's principal of one of our grammar schools. Three are on the town payroll, in public works; and Reggie Sawyer Jr., the son of the principal, is captain of the high-school football team and president of the senior class. And there're a couple of others who live here but work elsewhere. One's a TV newscaster in New York.

So you can't say this town's racist. That's the kind of thing I fight against. That, and dope, and child abuse. There's none of that here, either.

Well, I didn't mean there isn't any drugs. I meant child abuse. I'll be honest with you. Drugs are a bit of a problem. But we have a good antidrug program going. We're going to lick it.

But there's this kid, Wilfred Greene, from God knows where. I don't know if *he* even knows. He's now been identified as the stranger who'd come to town last Thursday, the day Sally Anders got killed.

He looks innocent. I don't know how to explain it. He's been identified as the stranger who's supposed to be the murderer, but I watch his amazement at being brought here from forty miles away and being made to explain his activities, describe his life-style, tell his purpose in passing through our town in the first place.

You'd think our town was sacrosanct, that you couldn't come here without a passport!

I sensed he was reaching out to me, trying to find some flotsam or jetsam in his unordered world that he could cling to. At this point, understand, he hadn't been accused of anything, charged with anything.

The most important part of my thinking was that it didn't really seem to dawn on him that he was going to be charged with murder. I mean, I've been a cop long enough to know that your act of innocence isn't going to fool a professional if you're guilty.

But, if that was true, then Wilfred Greene should be written up in books. For, if he was guilty, he was fooling *me*.

The chief came in, the chief and Captain Appleby and Jack Harris, our best detective. And Betty Mahler, our policewoman and secretary. They all were having trouble hiding their glee, and I wondered if Wilfred Greene could sense the change in atmosphere and fear for his life.

We went into the chief's office and sat the kid down, and the chief asked him point blank why he denied he'd been in town before.

"Well, Christ," the kid said, "I didn't know I had. I hit a lot of towns. Mostly I don't know their names. If you say I been here, I'll take your word for it."

"You came in off the turnpike and frightened a woman who was gardening in her front yard. You followed her into her house when she tried to look up a fictitious address for you. You going to say you've forgotten that?"

"Hey," Wilfred said agreeably, "if you wanna say that's what happened, it happened."

"And that afternoon, another woman found you in her backyard. What were you doing there?"

"I don't know. I don't remember it."

"She's willing to swear in court that you were in her backyard and when she wanted to know what you were doing there, you climbed over her rear fence into another backyard."

"Let her swear. I'm not going to deny it. So I was in somebody's backyard."

"What do you go into people's backyards for?"

Wilfred shrugged. "I dunno. To see what they look like."

"To see if there's anything you can steal."

"That's you saying that. I'm not saying anything." He looked at the lot of us in disbelief. "Christ, is that what you brought me all the way down here for? Because I was in some woman's backyard?"

"And that evening? What'd you do that evening?"

"Hell, I don't know. Slept under a car somewhere if it was raining, otherwise in the woods."

"You might forget that afternoon, but you aren't forgetting that evening. Not *that* evening! Not *that girl!*"

Wilfred picked up on "girl" like a truck hit him. "What girl?"

"The baby-sitter. In the big house kitty-corner to the pond."

"What house? What pond? What baby-sitter?"

"You going to deny you went prowling around a house that evening, around *another* backyard? And there was a young girl baby-sitting inside?"

He was starting to perspire. "What? I wasn't around no house and no baby-sitter. I don't know what you're talking about."

The chief leaned close. "Well, now, mister, we'll tell you what we're talking about. We're talking about murder, mister. We're talking about what you did to a little sixteen-year-old girl last Thursday night. Rape and murder, mister. We're talking rape and murder. And you're going to tell us about it."

Wilfred came so far out of his chair, Harris and I had to yank him back down and tell him to stay put. "But you're crazy!" he screamed. And I mean, he really screamed. But it was his eyes that were crazy. They were going around at us all and they were wild. He was looking for a smile or a wink, something that would tell him it was April Fools. But he knew the date wasn't April first and he knew we hadn't dragged him down here from Mystic Point for trespassing. We had him on something a lot bigger than that, something bigger than he'd ever dreamed.

"You're being held on suspicion of murder," the chief told him. "You have a right to remain silent and you have the right to an attorney. Anything you do say can be used in evidence against you." The chief gave him a card with his rights written on it and told him to read it aloud.

The guy did, in a voice that quavered.

"You understand your rights?" Hickey said.

"Listen," Wilfred pleaded, "what'm I supposed to've done? I don't understand any of this."

"You don't remember what you did last Thursday?"

"No, no, I don't." He was almost crying. "I don't even know where I *was* last Thursday."

"You want us to believe you don't know what you were doing three days ago?"

"Listen. Honest to God, I don't know where I was *one* day ago. I been hitching around, drifting around. Every day's alike, except if it's raining. I remember the rainy days longer. Every town's alike."

"And every baby-sitter's alike? That's what you want us to believe?"

He buried his face in his hands. "I don't know. I don't know what you're talking about. Somebody easy comes along, I'm not gonna knock it. But I don't push where I'm not wanted."

"She invited you. That's it, isn't it? She let you think she was willing, and when you found out she wasn't willing, you were too worked up. You couldn't help yourself. That's it, isn't it? She led you on?"

He lifted frightened eyes from his cupped hands. "Honest, I don't even know what you're talking about. When was this? You're saying this was last Thursday?"

"Thursday, May the seventh. You were here in town."

"I might've been. I don't know what towns I hit last Thursday. It's in and out, in and out. See what's there,

see the prospects, and move on. Last Thursday?" He
furrowed his brow.

"You came off the turnpike, and a woman was working
in her garden out by the road."

He lapsed for a moment into thought. "Yeah," he said.
"I remember her. Nice figure. Halter and shorts. I remember. She didn't like me looking at her. Some women
don't. She wanted to know what I wanted. I gave her a
phony address. I wanted to keep looking at her. I thought
she might warm up after a while. She went into the
house. I remember. I followed her. She didn't like that.
She didn't like finding the name and address weren't real
either. I figured she might report me, but I hadn't touched
her or done anything, so I didn't know what she could
report me about. And I went on my way."

"And then what did you do?"

He seemed genuinely trying to recall. "I checked out
the town. I don't truly remember whatever it was I did. I
walked the streets, looked in yards like you say, and I saw
enough cops on patrol to decide there wasn't any point in
hanging around. It was a nice, tidy town, well kept, well
patrolled. People would gang up on an outsider. You
couldn't divide and conquer, so to speak. You steal one
guy's bike, they'll all be after you, not just the guy you
stole it from. You know what I'm talking about? It's not
the kind of town you can do anything in. So I moved on."

"So you moved on," Chief Hickey said. "Like when?"

"I don't know. Midafternoon." He looked around with
those raised, helpless eyebrows. "Listen, believe me. I
remember now! The middle of the afternoon—middle to
late afternoon. I hiked back to the turnpike and hitched
out."

"Who gave you the ride?"

"Oh, Christ," he anguished, "you expect me to remember something like *that*?"

"It's your alibi, mister. You'd better remember."

He buried his face and dug his palms into his eyes. "Oh
God, oh God. What'd I do? Where'd I go?" He lifted his
face and stared at the ceiling. "Thursday night. Thursday,

Thursday." His face brightened. "I know where I was last Thursday night! I was in *jail!*"

We all looked at each other. I hate to admit it—our chagrin at the possibility our suspect might be innocent. It ought to fill our hearts with joy—an innocent man has not been wrongly convicted. But we all stared in horror at the thought. We had our man, dammit! There wasn't anybody else. There couldn't be anybody else. We didn't want him to be innocent. We wanted him to be guilty!

And I'm ashamed to have to say that.

Chief Hickey was the first to recover. "You say you were in jail?" He spoke very quietly and he tried not to lose his scowl, but if ever I saw a man pale around the gills, he was that man. Three hundred people were outside on the Green, electrified with the expectation that vengeance was about to be wrought. And here was the man we all lusted for and slavered over, saying he'd been in jail at the time Sally Anders had been murdered.

The chief said, "In jail where?"

"Jeez," Wilfred said, feeling a little better at the consternation he'd sown, but still sweating rivets. "I don't know. Up the line."

The chief leaned on the arms of Wilfred's chair. That's how close he put his face to Wilfred's. "Don't feed me your 'I don't know' crap. What were you in jail for? What'd you do *after* you claim you left here?"

Wilfred rubbed his face with a dirty handkerchief. "I hitched a ride on east. Late afternoon. I could tell nothing was gonna happen here. A guy gave me a lift to where he turned off, and I rode into the center of town with him to check the place out. I was hungry so I looked around for something I might be able to trade in for a meal, or someone I might be able to charm into treating me to dinner, or someone might be leaving a purse lying around.

"I tried the shopping center and, well, I picked up a purse. A woman had left it in her shopping cart getting something off the shelves. But my timing was bad. She

saw me and I had to run for it and, just my luck, there
was an off-duty cop in the store and he got me.

"So, like I say, I got booked and thrown in the slammer
because I couldn't post any bond, and that's where I spent
the night."

"Then what?"

"In the morning the woman came down, but she wouldn't
press charges and the cops took me to the edge of town
and turned me loose with a warning not to come back."

"And what town was this?"

"Christ, I don't know," Wilfred said miserably. "All I
know is the cop who arrested me was named Farrell.
Mike Farrell. And I never met a meaner sonovabitch."

The rest of us looked at each other. There was a sergeant named Farrell on the force in Clinton Center.

We put Wilfred in a cell and the chief took a deep
breath and phoned the station in Clinton Center. It read
like he said. A vagrant identified as Wilfred Greene,
description matching, was picked up by Sergeant Farrell
on a theft charge at quarter of seven on the evening of
Thursday, May seventh. He'd spent the night in jail there
and been set loose at eleven o'clock the following morning. They had his fingerprints, if we wanted to check
fingerprints, his picture if we wanted to see his picture.

Chief Hickey said fine, we'd send over for a copy of the
photograph to verify the ID. But when he put down the
phone we all knew Wilfred not only had been telling the
truth, he had the greatest alibi in the world. Absolutely
the greatest!

"There goes our case," Jack Harris said. "Sonovabitch.
I'd've bet my life we had the right guy!"

"Yeah," Appleby said and gestured toward the Green.
"And what're we going to tell the crowd out there? They
smell blood and they aren't going to be happy going home
without their pound of flesh."

"Maybe Reverend Wallace can give them a talk on
mercy," Harris said. "I could use one myself about now."

"How'll we tell 'em? Go over in a squad car with a
bullhorn and then drive like hell?"

"We shouldn't commit ourselves to anything," I said, "until we match our boy with the picture Clinton Center's got. You never can tell."

"You're grasping for straws," Nat Appleby told me. "We all know we're holding an empty bag."

"And it looks bad for the police department," Jack Harris said. "The town's really gonna be on our backs now." He turned. "Right, Chief? You think the board of police commissioners will knuckle under and clean house?"

"That's not what's worrying me," Chief Hickey said. "That's not where it's at."

"What do you mean? Where *is* it at?"

"Do you realize," Hickey said, and looked at us all. "That if the stranger didn't do it, the Anders girl was raped and murdered by someone here in town?"

Sunday–Thursday, May 10–14

Chief Hickey, for all you might want to say about his brain power matched against the Yale professors, artists, musicians and writers in town—that whole intellectual crowd—nevertheless saw quicker through to the heart of the matter than anybody else that Sunday night when they had to turn Wilfred Greene loose and ship him back to Mystic Point. Chief Hickey was the first to realize that, once they let go of Wilfred Greene, they were conceding that the murderer of pretty young Sally Anders wasn't a rapacious stranger, about whom it's always easy to believe the worst; it was someone in the group, an asp in their own bosom. The killer was one of their own.

As I say, he realized it that night, even before they let Wilfred Greene go. And in the back of his mind, he was frantically grasping at some straw, some way to hold Wilfred, some way the unwholesome stranger might have tricked them, appeared to be two places at once. How convenient it would have been if Wilfred had been guilty! The case could have been wrapped up, the horror laid to rest, and life could go on. It was not to be. Wilfred had been proven innocent and the mystery remained. But

89

Hickey wasn't surprised. He'd been a cop too many years
ever to expect an easy solution.

What *did* enter his mind—something he wouldn't mention if *he* were writing this report, but something he
privately acknowledged he was thinking about, all the
while arrangements were being made to spirit Wilfred out
of town, alive and in one piece, was: Who, in the slime
and grime, yes, and *crime*—for there's that too—in this
town, raped and murdered one of our nice young girls?

And he raked through his mind all the time this other
business was going on. Because that was the first question
anyone would ask him. "If the stranger didn't do it, Chief,
who did?" Especially that question would be directed to
him by the police commissioners. He was their answering
machine. He'd been hired, as all police chiefs are hired,
to produce the "goods" and make the police commissioners look good—make the town look good, of course, but,
for God's sake, don't spill egg on the commissioners.
Don't let them think they made a bad choice when they
pinned on your gold badge.

And Chief Hickey's mind was sorting through everything he could think of to do with anybody in town who'd
committed any kind of a crime. And he couldn't think of
anyone!

Oh, not that a raft of names didn't come to mind: of the
cheats, the thieves, the freeloaders, the reprobates, the
welchers, the parasites, the wife swappers, the adulterers,
the sex offenders, the two suspected child molesters,
the homosexuals and lesbians—more of both than were
suspected—the malingerers, the sick, the maimed, the
diseased, the kooks, the wife beaters! Chief Hickey had
more such names in his memory bank than most people
have friends. But never in his experience with any of the
town's known malefactors had he sensed, beneath their
surface sins, the soul of a creature who would wantonly
rape, brutalize and murder a girl like Sally Anders.

What bothered Chief Hickey the most was that he
should *have to* thumb through their names. It showed
him uncertain both as to their character and his own.

Mostly it was his own that tormented him. If one of these people had done such a deed, how could *he*, Herbert Hickey, possessed of his training and skill, endowed with his ego and pride, have overlooked the signs? How could such a flagrant criminal have escaped his notice? His oversight had caused the death of this young girl. It made him responsible.

On the other hand, if it hadn't been one of the names on the blotter, that made it someone who'd never been called to the attention of the police; one of the upright, "noble" citizens in town, perhaps a community leader? That was an even worse consideration—that a murderer so heinous and beyond salvation could walk the streets of Crockford in convivial intercourse, fooling his confreres and friends, but fooling *Hickey* as well!

Chief Hickey might be faulted for assuming too much blame, but he did have an overdeveloped sense of responsibility, a tendency to accept the welfare of the town as his personal obligation. It was one of the reasons the Board of Police Commissioners hired him. His sense of duty meant more to them than his intellect. And they could, by the pressure of their own weight, maximize his sense of duty, leaving them assured that their town was the best-policed town in Connecticut. And, in honesty to the Police Commission, self-aggrandizement wasn't their sole aim. They really meant, and wanted their town to boast the *best* police department in the State of Connecticut.

And they were as appalled at the murder of Sally Anders, in the heart of the "best and finest town in Connecticut," as was Herb Hickey. And they were even more at a loss, for they could not accept, as Herb agonizingly did, the idea that a member of *this society*, that an inhabitant of this "best of all towns" could have committed one of the most heinous crimes known to man.

The rest of the town was equally slow to grasp the significance of Wilfred Greene's innocence. At first the talk in the marketplace revolved around what *other* strangers could have come into town, committed the crime and made an escape. Then, slowly, but only slowly, a suggestion here, a query there, the possibility was put forth that the murderer wasn't a stranger at all. Perhaps it was *one of us!*

That suggestion was still only in the half-formed phase until Thursday, May 14, when the *Shoreline News* came out with an editorial that exploded in town like nitroglycerin. Who Did It? was the title, and it read like this:

One week ago tonight, sometime between eight and twelve midnight, someone in this town, some twisted, demented, apology for a human being, approached the home of Charles and Pamela Parker at 325 North Ferry Street. Inside that home, unknowing and innocent, slept two little boys, Richard, 4, and David, 2½. Watching over them was the Parker baby-sitter for the evening, 16-year-old Sally Anders, a junior in the high school. She'd brought her books with her to do her homework while the children slept.

But she didn't do any homework that night.

Because that twisted, evil, demented human being, whose soul should better have been roasting in hell, came to the door and entered the house. And what he did to Sally Anders defies description. To put it as painlessly as possible, what he did was rape and murder this young girl, drag her body out into the field beyond the house, and cast it away.

Thankfully, we shall never know the thoughts that went through Sally Anders' mind when this embodiment of evil made known his intentions. We shall never know the horror of her experience. We shall never hear her cries for help as the monster cruelly beat down her defenses, attacked her body and then, to make sure she never revealed to anyone what he had done to her, beat in her skull with a hammer until she was dead.

And when he was finished with his foul deed, this inexcusable mockery of a human being redonned his cloak of gentility and, with an air of innocence, re-

sumed his habit of walking our streets, sharing our
friendships, conversing with us, patting our *own* young
daughters on the head, and making a lie of everything we hold dear.

For, members of this friendly community of Crockford, this town of which we are so proud, and which
we are so pleased to inhabit, understand one thing! A
murderer walks among us. A foul, evil creature lurks
in this town, hiding his debauched mind behind a
winsome face. Here, among us, lives the embodiment of Dorian Gray, a true copy of Oscar Wilde's
creation whose beguiling expression and charm of
manner disguises a soul of evil.

That we could harbor such a fiend and not know it is
terror enough. That any man could stoop so low
defies belief. But it has happened once and we must
make sure it never happens again. We cannot wait
until the next full moon, when the werewolf might
claim another victim. We must not ever let this frightful crime be repeated.

He knows who he is, this murderer in our midst, this
asp in our bosom. Let us urge that he think about his
crime, that he come forth and confess, that an innate
sense of decency will move him to warn us before his
madness drives him to strike again.

Surely, such a man cannot relish his deed. He must
be as appalled at his actions as the rest of us.

Confess! If pity lie in your heart, confess!

Meanwhile, it is up to the rest of us to keep our eyes
open, to catch the slip that, sooner or later, all criminals make. Perhaps it's a look in the eye, an open
window to a black heart. Perhaps it will be a furtive
glance, the signal of guilt, or a lecherous stare at a
well-developed young woman. One way or another
the villain will betray himself. One way or another he
must be caught.

Our town must be made safe again.

Thursday May 14

ST. BARTHOLOMEW'S CHURCH MEMBERSHIP COM-
MITTEE (4:00 P.M.) PRESENT: Dorothy Meskill (Chair-
man); Jessie Mund (Secretary); Carole Wayne; Robert
Saltzer. ABSENT: Darwin Lane.

DOROTHY MESKILL
Darwin sends his regrets. He has a doctor's appointment this afternoon.

JESSIE MUND
Did any of you read Phil Croft's editorial today? I
mean, I think he's got no right to write things like that!
He's trying to scare the wits out of us.

ROBERT SALTZER
That's Phil. He *does* tend to overdo the emotion bit.

94

JESSIE MUND

I don't think he's being emotional. I think he's deliberately trying to scare us. If it isn't bad enough what happened a week ago, he wants us to think it might happen again!

CAROLE WAYNE

You think it won't?

JESSIE MUND

What're you talking about? You act like you believe him—the idea that somebody in town—

CAROLE WAYNE

You *don't* believe him?

JESSIE MUND

Well, of course not. I mean . . . you know. There's nobody in this town—

DOROTHY MESKILL

That's just what *I* thought. Nobody in this town. But when I read the editorial—

ROBERT SALTZER

Oh, hell, if it wasn't that kid they arrested—the one they had to let go—who else could it be but someone in

town? Why shouldn't it be? What's so wonderful about
this town? It happens everywhere else in the world. What
makes us so sacrosanct?

JESSIE MUND
You mean you were thinking that way too? It wasn't just
the editorial?

ROBERT SALTZER
I think we *all* have to think that way.

DOROTHY MESKILL
The editorial shook me up, I admit. It made me realize
what I think I should have realized before now. Except
that I saw that Wilfred Greene lad. He gave me a fright
that still gives me the shivers. He was in the house with
me—in the kitchen, and we were all alone. And I could
smell evil in him. I don't know how to explain it, but I
could *smell* it. I couldn't get that young man out of my
mind. I think that's why I didn't think about anybody in
town being guilty. I couldn't get it out of my head that,
somehow, it could only be him. Of course that doesn't
make much sense.

ROBERT SALTZER
Yeah, but if the police had used their heads, they
should've known he didn't do it. Because if he was going
to do that sort of thing, he'd have done it to you, Dorothy.
Right there, that morning. Like you say, he had the
perfect opportunity.

DOROTHY MESKILL

Yes. I hadn't thought of that. That's true. And if I'd screamed—there in the kitchen, in the back of the house—I don't know who could've heard me.

CAROLE WAYNE

It'd be better not to scream and just do what he wanted.

JESSIE MUND

Sally shouldn't have screamed. Maybe she'd be alive today if she hadn't screamed.

ROBERT SALTZER

That's another thing that bothers me about the editorial. Phil claims Sally screamed. How does he know that?

CAROLE WAYNE

He's assuming. You could read between the lines he was making up most of it for effect.

JESSIE MUND

Especially trying to say it's somebody here in town.

DOROTHY MESKILL

Well, if you don't think it was somebody in town, who do you think did it?

JESSIE MUND
Anybody! Just because it wasn't the man they caught
doesn't mean it wasn't someone just like him who they
didn't catch.

ROBERT SALTZER
Somebody from out of town who just *happens* to knock
on any door, just happens to find a baby-sitter all alone
and goes berserk?

JESSIE MUND
It's a thief—from out of town. They come down from
New Haven all the time. It's a nice-looking house, close to
the turnpike, the door's unlocked, and he walks in.

ROBERT SALTZER
But nothing was stolen.

JESSIE MUND
He got distracted. A lot of those robbers rape their
victims. You read about it all the time.

ROBERT SALTZER
But when they're through, they don't forget to take the
family jewels with them.

JESSIE MUND
Robert, I'm not going to argue with you. You always
put up these ridiculous arguments.

CAROLE WAYNE
Speaking of screams, did anybody hear her? I've never
heard the subject mentioned.

JESSIE MUND
What about the two little boys? They'd have heard her
if she screamed.

CAROLE WAYNE
And the old woman in the house across the street.

ROBERT SALTZER
Mrs. Tyler? She's deaf. And if she was in bed— How
about up where you are, Dorothy? You're not so far away.

DOROTHY MESKILL
I asked Ed about it. That fact was bothering me too. He
was correcting papers in the study with the window open
but he didn't hear a thing. So I don't think she screamed
at all.

ROBERT SALTZER
The noise from turnpike traffic—maybe he couldn't have
heard her if she did scream.

DOROTHY MESKILL
But the study faces away from the turnpike, down
toward the Parker house, and it's only two or three hundred
yards. I think a scream could be heard.

ROBERT SALTZER
Unless her windows were closed and she was already
dead when he brought her out of the house.

JESSIE MUND
Robert, for heaven's sake, do you have to be so gruesome?

DOROTHY MESKILL
Yes, Robert. And we do have some membership names
to consider.

JESSIE MUND
Yes, except I don't understand one thing. Do you *all*
think the man who murdered Sally lives here in town?
(All nod.) You mean, someone we all know?

ROBERT SALTZER
Maybe *some* of us know him.

JESSIE MUND
Like one of us? Like, maybe, one of us right here in
this room?

ROBERT SALTZER
Well, since I'm the only male present and the murder
was obviously committed by a man, I'd prefer that you
turn your attention elsewhere.

DOROTHY MESKILL
It's probably not somebody any of us knows. It's probably one of the lower-class people in town. (*Pause*) You don't agree, Robert?

ROBERT SALTZER
What?

DOROTHY MESKILL
I noticed a note of disapproval in your expression.

ROBERT SALTZER
I was just thinking how easy it is to lay blame elsewhere—especially on people of less education or intelligence, on people less like ourselves.

CAROLE WAYNE
You mean you think someone like *us* did it?

ROBERT SALTZER
I only mean that if you went to the bars and bowling alleys in town, visited the blue-collar places, the people there would probably be wondering who, from some *other* group—maybe ours—could have done such a thing. I've always thought how much easier it is to imagine Dracula coming from Transylvania than from Westchester County.

JESSIE MUND
Well, if it's somebody from around here, he'd have to be a maniac, that's all I can say. And we don't have any in town.

CAROLE WAYNE
How about Clyde Worth?

JESSIE MUND
Clyde? Oh, Carole, be sensible. Clyde's no maniac.

CAROLE WAYNE
But he's strange. He's not normal.

JESSIE MUND
But he's pleasant and friendly. And, besides, what's he do that's so strange? He minds his own business and takes walks.

CAROLE WAYNE
Takes walks? That's putting it mildly. He must walk thirty miles a day.

ROBERT SALTZER
It gives him a trim figure at least. Maybe I should try it.

CAROLE WAYNE
No matter what road you drive on, no matter how far out from the center of town you might be, you never know when you're going to come across Clyde walking along the roadside.

ROBERT SALTZER
Maybe he likes the scenery.

CAROLE WAYNE
And God knows what he might find out there that the rest of us miss because we go by too fast.

ROBERT SALTZER
You mean some couple hidden in the grass, doing something they shouldn't?

DOROTHY MESKILL
Robert, you have an evil mind.

JESSIE MUND
He sees things. He finds things. He found a book lying beside the road. In good condition. And he gave it to the library.

CAROLE WAYNE
But he doesn't work, he can't support himself. Where does he live?

DOROTHY MESKILL

In what used to be the Tinker Shop. Steve Polinski lets him stay there. Him and his cats.

CAROLE WAYNE

Steve Polinski? What's he charge him for rent?

DOROTHY MESKILL

No rent. No nothing.

ROBERT SALTZER

Including no electricity and no plumbing.

CAROLE WAYNE

What's got into Steve? Everything he buys he turns into money. The barber shop? He made it into three shops—and got more rent for each than Bill Dormer was paying for cutting hair.

JESSIE MUND

And Steve Polinski wouldn't be letting Clyde Worth use his property if Clyde was a maniac.

CAROLE WAYNE

I'm not saying he's a maniac. I'm saying he's *strange*. He doesn't work, he hasn't any money, and he gets his clothes from raiding the Good Will collection bin.

ROBERT SALTZER

You hear the story Marion Kleves tells? She was dumping some clothes into the Good Will bin when she felt this hand in there. Clyde was inside, keeping warm and sleeping, I guess. She says she jumped three feet.

DOROTHY MESKILL

I heard Marion was so furious she wanted him arrested.

ROBERT SALTZER

That's the one thing about people who're strange. You don't know *what* they'll do. That's what makes them strange. They can go along being almost normal, then, for reasons only they can understand, they'll do something extraordinary!

JESSIE MUND

Like murder Sally Anders—that's what you're saying?

ROBERT SALTZER

Not saying anything of the kind. All I'm suggesting is that, if we're looking for someone in town to be a murderer, I wouldn't pass up looking at Clyde. Unless there's specific evidence pointing to someone else, all we've got to go on is that Clyde's the only one in town who *might* have committed the murder. That's not to say he did, but right now he's the only possibility.

JESSIE MUND

You mean, so far as *you* know.

ROBERT SALTZER

So far as I know. That's true. And who's your choice?

JESSIE MUND

I told you! It's that Wilfred Greene. Or somebody like him. It's a gen-*u*-ine criminal, a jailbird, a sex offender. And he doesn't come from *our* town.

(*Enter Walter Wallace, minister of St. Bartholomew's Church*)

WALTER WALLACE

Sorry if I'm late. I was attending the choir rehearsal. I wanted— It's different now. I'm afraid a joyfulness is gone. You understand what I mean.

DOROTHY MESKILL

Sally's was the best voice. You seldom get a voice like hers.

WALTER WALLACE

She and Peggy. The two together. It was an experience. I've never heard two voices more in tune. Like the girls themselves! Those are rare occurrences. I'm sure they didn't realize themselves how rare such relationships are.

CAROLE WAYNE

Was Peggy at rehearsal?

WALTER WALLACE
No. She's resigned from the choir, I'm sorry to say.

JESSIE MUND
We've been talking about . . . what happened. What's
your view, Father? There's talk . . . Phil Croft's editorial.
Do *you* think Sally was killed by somebody here in town?

WALTER WALLACE
I find I don't know what to think. It's easy to lay the
blame for what happened on strangers. That's why we do it.
It's so *easy*! But the evidence indicates— Well, I don't know
what to say. I've talked to Chief Hickey. The police are
working on it, but they're in the dark. We're all in the dark.

ROBERT SALTZER
Clyde Worth's been mentioned as a possibility. You
know him. Could he have done such a thing?

WALTER WALLACE
Clyde? Hmm. I hadn't really thought about anybody. I
suppose it's possible. I've talked with him from time to
time, but I confess I don't understand him. He doesn't
strike me as the type, to tell the truth. But how well do I
know him? I sense areas in Clyde that I can't probe. He's
not quite like the rest of us.

CAROLE WAYNE
Can you think of anybody else who isn't "quite like the
rest of us"?

ROBERT SALTZER
Can you see Clyde Worth *doing* such a thing?

WALTER WALLACE
I wish I could give you an answer. Who knows the
blackness of the human soul? I think I understand a little
about God. I think I grasp His message for the world. I
know I understand what He wants from us. I *know* how
we are to respond to His will. But His methods, His
means of making His designs manifest are very subtle and
very deep. Even the scholars cannot fully understand the
significance of His doings.

DOROTHY MESKILL
Well, now, like what?

WALTER WALLACE
Like what happened to Sally Anders. In what way was
this a part of His Design?

JESSIE MUND
That was the work of the Devil. The Devil got the
upper hand there.

CAROLE WAYNE
Is that what you believe, Father? That Sally's death was
the work of the Devil?

WALTER WALLACE

I think whatever devil exists, exists within our own souls. No, I don't believe Sally's death was the work of the Devil.

CAROLE WAYNE

Then what? Why did such a thing happen?

WALTER WALLACE

My own personal belief is that it was a part of God's Scheme of Things, a scheme the Purpose of Which is for Good, but a scheme, by means of which this Purpose is advanced, I cannot truthfully say. All I can promise you, my friends, is that whatever happens in this world is by the Will of God, and the Goodness of it lies in God's Cosmic Scheme for the universe and will only be made manifest as the future unfolds.

JESSIE MUND

You don't make me feel good at all.

WALTER WALLACE

We cannot be made to "feel good" by what happens to us in this world. All that can make us feel good is that we believe in God's worth and wisdom, love and devotion, and that we walk steadfastly in the path He has laid out for us. This is where I walk. This is what makes me happy. This is where we should all walk together and be happy.

However, I think this isn't the purpose of this meeting. We're supposed to be discussing the effects of our membership drive.

Thursday May 14

POLICE COMMISSION MEETING—EXECUTIVE SESSION (8:00 P.M.) PRESENT: Hugh McCormick (Chairman); Donald Harding; Charles Parker; Chief Herbert Hickey; Detective Jack Harris; Patrolwoman Elizabeth Mahler (Recording Secretary).

HUGH McCORMICK
I don't have to tell you what we're all thinking and feeling. It's been a week now and we're all in the dark. That's right, isn't it, Herb?

CHIEF HICKEY
I'm afraid so, sir. We're convinced it's got to be someone here in town, but so far Jack hasn't been able to come up with a lead. Right, Jack?

DETECTIVE HARRIS
We've tried to track her movements that day—see if
she did anything out of the ordinary. Did she talk to
somebody or meet somebody not in her normal pattern?
So far we haven't come up with anything.

DONALD HARDING
You got any clues as to what time it happened? Right
after she put the kids to bed? Late in the evening? Can
we pinpoint when? Also, is it true that nobody heard her
scream? Phil Croft's editorial talks about her screaming.
Did anybody hear her scream?

DETECTIVE HARRIS
No, sir, Mr. Harding. We haven't found anybody. And
we've investigated that angle pretty thoroughly.

DONALD HARDING
Like, how thoroughly? Just what've you done?

HUGH McCORMICK
Do we have to go into detail, Don? If Jack says—

DONALD HARDING
I'm a commissioner. People are stopping me on the
streets, quizzing me at parties, wanting to know what
we're doing. They want concrete answers, and I'm going
to give them concrete answers.

DETECTIVE HARRIS

Mrs. Tyler, who lives across the road from Mr. Parker, is the nearest person. We've talked to her. Next nearest would be the Whitesides, who live up above, but they were out, of course. They were at the concert with Mr. and Mrs. Parker. Then, south down North Ferry Street from the Parkers, down near Route 1 there's the Brownings and the Flynns and two other houses where the people were away, and around the corner, there's the silversmith's out on Route 1. But that was closed at that hour and nobody was in the place.

Then, behind Mr. Parker, there're four people living in the old gatehouse that belonged to the Sedley mansion before it was converted into a school and burned down during World War Two—a young couple named Tattersol, and two women, a phys ed instructor at the high school, Marcia Van Doren, and an artist, Nancy Trowbridge. There's only a broken-down fence between the properties down from the Parkers' barn, and the Parkers' patio, off the kitchen, isn't thirty yards away. All four people in the gatehouse were home that night, but all four claim they never heard a thing.

You go up North Ferry Street past the pond, and there're the Meskills and the Doudens, the Gordons beyond the Meskills, and the Jacksons nearest the Doudens. If Mrs. Tyler and the four people in the gatehouse didn't hear anything, there's not much chance anybody else did. But we hit every house on North Ferry Street, on Peach Lane, on North State, and Siddons Street. Every house, sir. And nobody who was home that night saw or heard anything out of the usual.

CHARLES PARKER

I talked to everybody around there myself, and he's right. Nobody could tell me a thing.

DETECTIVE HARRIS
We tend to think she didn't scream. We don't see how
she could've without somebody hearing her.

HUGH McCORMICK
Unless she did her screaming inside the house with the
windows closed? What about that, Jack?

DETECTIVE HARRIS
We don't think that could've happened without her
waking the kids—Mr. Parker's little boys.

HUGH McCORMICK
But you can't tell about kids. I mean, with all due
respect, Charley—your kids could've waked and gone back
to sleep and forgotten it, or they might be afraid to say
what they heard.

CHARLES PARKER
With "all due respect," Hugh, that's not what happened. Pam and I, together and separately, have both had
them tell us everything they can remember about that
night. Do you think, for God's sake, that we aren't doing
everything we can think of in this case? But all they can
tell us—all they know—is she let them watch a nature
program on TV and put them to bed. That would have
been eight o'clock, because I checked the TV listings
and matched it with what they saw. I haven't just been
sitting, twiddling my thumbs this past week, if you want
to know. I've gone over with my kids everything that
happened that night, everything they can remember.

I've tried to get out of them things they didn't *know* they'd remembered. But it's a blank, gentlemen. It's a blank. Sally sat with them through the program, she put them to bed, and that's all they know until we were waking them up in the middle of the night, asking them questions.

HUGH McCORMICK
They do remember that much? They remember being waked up?

CHARLES PARKER
David's forgotten it, but Richard recalls a great commotion and people asking him about Sally. That's all he could tell me. He doesn't know yet that Sally's dead.

DONALD HARDING
So it had to happen between eight and midnight? Can we cut it any closer than that?

DETECTIVE HARRIS
The autopsy—the food in her stomach—the pathologist who did it thinks death around ten o'clock would be it. But he wouldn't want to go on record.

HUGH McCORMICK
That's a pretty safe guess, I'd think. Even without an autopsy.

DONALD HARDING

Her books were neatly stacked on the dining-room table, I hear. She hadn't started her homework yet. Maybe it's closer to eight than ten?

CHIEF HICKEY

The sun didn't set until after eight. We don't think anybody would have approached the girl before dark. We think nine o'clock to be the earliest time.

CHARLES PARKER

She'd likely watch television for a while before settling down to any homework. My wife thinks she wouldn't, but I think she would—stall off the evil moment. At least if she was anything like me. I don't think the fact her books weren't touched is a clue of any kind.

DONALD HARDING

Well, we've got to explore every possibility.

CHARLES PARKER

More important is finding out whether this was accident or design. What do you think, Herb? You think this was done by someone who *knew* she was baby-sitting for us that night, or that someone just happened by?

CHIEF HICKEY

We have to think it's more likely someone *knew* she was there and came with the intent to take advantage of the fact she was alone.

HUGH McCORMICK
Especially if it was somebody here in town, like Phil Crofts claims in his editorial. You think that's the case, Herb, that the killer is someone in town?

CHIEF HICKEY
To tell you the truth, since we no longer have a Wilfred Greene coming to town, spotting her and following her, the only way it makes sense is to figure it was done by someone who lives here, who knows who she is and knew she was baby-sitting at Mr. Parker's house last Thursday.

DONALD HARDING
That doesn't make any sense to me, if you want to know. If somebody in town had a hankering for the girl, why wouldn't this have happened a long time ago? Anywhere—out in the woods, in his own house, behind the school, in the back seat of his car? Why only when she's baby-sitting and a couple of little kids are sleeping close by?

CHARLES PARKER
You mean *kidnap* the girl?

DONALD HARDING
If he's so hot for her that he'll rape and kill her, why not? Why the hell not?

CHARLES PARKER

You have a point, Don. Why the hell would he do it where and when he did? He could have picked so many better places! Somewhere else, where nobody could have heard her if she screamed. Then he mightn't have had to kill her. What about that, Herb? Have you thought about that?

CHIEF HICKEY

We've thought about it.

HUGH McCORMICK

You think he killed her to keep her from screaming?

CHIEF HICKEY

We think the most likely reason he killed her was because she knew who he was.

HUGH McCORMICK

Meaning . . . one of us? Not some cocaine addict from God knows what part of town?

CHIEF HICKEY

Crack addicts aren't interested in sex. They're only interested in crack. We think it was someone she knew because we don't know why he'd kill her otherwise. In most cases, you don't have to kill a woman to rape her. She doesn't have the strength to resist, so you just rape her. There's no reason to kill her in the bargain.

HUGH McCORMICK
. God, what a sexist statement! I'm only glad we're in executive session.

CHIEF HICKEY
I'm only trying to explain facts. Most rapists are driven by the need for sexual gratification—release. They hanker. They dream. They aspire. And, in extreme cases—like the crackpot who tried to kill President Reagan to impress Jody Foster—some sexually driven person will do *anything* to satisfy the inner drive. Rape is usually enough. Sally Anders was raped. That should have been enough. It wasn't. He had to kill her as well. We can understand why he would rape. More people in this town than you know can do something like that. But to murder the victim *after* the rape is something entirely different. That's not sex, that's fear.

This is why we believe that Sally recognized the man and he realized he had to kill her to keep his identity secret.

DONALD HARDING
To attack an innocent girl when she's baby-sitting, when there are children sleeping close by, when neighbors can hear her screams, when she knows who you are, and to kill her to keep her from screaming and telling? Anybody who could do that would be a maniac!

CHIEF HICKEY
That's the view *we* take. That's who we're seeking.

DONALD HARDING
A maniac? Here? We don't have any!

HUGH McCORMICK
What about Clyde Worth?

DONALD HARDING
Clyde Worth? What're you talking about, Hugh. He's
no maniac.

HUGH McCORMICK
Do you know where he lives? How he lives? Have you
talked to him recently?

DONALD HARDING
There's nothing to talk to Clyde Worth about. Except
maybe the weather. What about it?

HUGH McCORMICK
Have you seen that pigpen he lives in—what used to be
the Tinker Shop until Les Hubbard died? I was over there
last week with the first selectman and Dr. Allen, the
health officer. Talk about the Collyer brothers! You have
to weave your way between stacks of newspapers standing
shoulder high. There are kitty-litter trays tucked in between. He's got thirteen cats—according to Frank Folger's count, and he's first selectman, so I'll accept his
figure. The room reeks with cat dung. It's lit by candles
in holders Clyde puts on top of his stacks of newspapers

so he can see his way. He's got no electricity, no plumbing—I mean by that, no *toilet*. He gets some veterans' benefits and food stamps. I'll say for him, he doesn't beg, and he doesn't complain, and he takes good care of those cats. He looks after them better than he looks after himself.

But if there's an oddball in town, Clyde's the one.

CHARLES PARKER

Come on, Hugh, you can't think Clyde could be involved in this. He's no sex maniac.

HUGH McCORMICK

The trouble with people like Clyde is, you can't ever know what they are. You and I, Charles, all of us in this room, almost all of us in this town—all of us law-abiding citizens at least—we *know* ourselves and we *know* each other. Law-abiding citizens have boundaries that enclose them. There is a limit to what we will do, and we all know what those limits are—what we will fight for, what we will die for, what we will betray for. We all live in the same lifeboat.

The disturbing thing about Clyde, Charles, is that, because he doesn't conform, we can't predict exactly how or if his behavior will conform.

CHARLES PARKER

I still say Clyde is totally incapable. I can't even imagine him raping, let alone killing, Sally Anders.

HUGH McCORMICK

One thing, though, Charles. You don't know *what* the meekest soul is capable of until he's been driven over the edge. That's the scary thing about people who aren't quite right in the head. You don't know their depths. I know *your* depth, Charley, old man. I know just how much evil you're capable of. But not Clyde Worth. I don't know how much evil may lie in him.

DONALD HARDING

Very fancy lecture, Hugh. You make us all want to study psychiatry. But you aren't doing a damned thing to enlighten us. Tell me now, Herb, do you think Clyde Worth is guilty of killing Sally Anders?

CHIEF HICKEY

Well, no. We don't have any evidence against him.

DONALD HARDING

Oh, damn, the literal nature of the police mentality! I'm not saying, do you think Clyde *did* it, I'm saying, do you think, knowing what you know of the man, his ills and weaknesses, that he could *possibly* have raped and murdered Sally Anders?

CHIEF HICKEY

No, not really. Of course, that's only an opinion. I have no evidence.

DONALD HARDING
What evidence *do* you have? You and Detective Harris?

CHIEF HICKEY
We have to think it's somebody who, like you said,
doesn't have restrictions on his mind—a person who can
lose his head in certain situations.

DONALD HARDING
Sexual situations?

CHIEF HICKEY
We find that this is an area where people—men in
particular—are least able to control their emotions, are
least able to act rationally.

HUGH McCORMICK
You're beating around the bush, Herb. If it isn't Clyde,
who've you got in mind?

CHIEF HICKEY
The point is, we don't have *anybody*. Clyde is an "iffy."
We don't know what Clyde will do. But so far as we've
been able to track him, it doesn't add up. Joe Norrell—
has the gas station/grocery at the corner of Maplewood
and Stonehill Road—claims Clyde walked in at ten o'clock
that night and bought a root beer. That's a good five
miles from Mr. Parker's home, and he had to be walking. I mean, maybe you can prove he stole a car and

drove back and murdered Sally, but that's the stuff you
only put in detective stories. You don't do it that way
in real life.

DONALD HARDING
But you think it's going to be some kind of maniac?

CHIEF HICKEY
We think it has to be someone who's out of whack
somehow.

CHARLES PARKER
And who in town, if it isn't Clyde?

DONALD HARDING
What about . . . Reggie Sawyer?

CHARLES PARKER
Reggie Sawyer? You're kidding.

DONALD HARDING
What's kidding about it? Tell me—what's so kidding?

CHARLES PARKER

Reggie Sawyer is the star and captain of the high-school football team, he's president of the senior class, he's a top student, he's got scholarships to three Ivy League schools, his father's a soloist in the Crockford Congregational Church choir and principal of the Dudley Bishop Grammar School. That's what's kidding!

DONALD HARDING

And he's black!

CHARLES PARKER

So?

DONALD HARDING

So, did you also know that, back when he was in grammar school, the Anders let him come over and play with Sally on two or three occasions? Inviting a boy to come over and play with a girl?

CHARLES PARKER

The Sawyers were living on State Street at the time. They were neighbors.

DONALD HARDING

And the Anders are very liberal, and they'd bend over backwards to invite a black boy to play with their white daughter.

CHARLES PARKER

He was a *neighbor.*

DONALD HARDING

And he was a *boy*! What would they invite a boy over to play with their daughter for? Unless it was because he was black?

HUGH McCORMICK

What're you suggesting, Don? That there was some kind of continuing relationship?

DONALD HARDING

I'm saying a seed might have been planted.

CHIEF HICKEY

I don't think it's anything like that. We have book on a lot of kids in this town—the bad ones. We know who's doing what, even if we can't bring charges. And there's never been a word against Reggie Sawyer.

DONALD HARDING

And I'm not trying to say he's done anything wrong. I'm just saying we're looking for somebody who doesn't have the controls on him that Hugh was talking about. Somebody who's not "one of us." And all I'm saying is, you know about black people. They're oversexed. They don't have our values. They've got big cocks and—

HUGH McCORMICK
Now let's watch our language and our insinuations—

DONALD HARDING
Hell, I'm not saying anything. This is executive session.
We can let our hair down here. This is a murder case,
damn it. We have to say what we think. We're all
men—

HUGH McCORMICK
Our recording secretary is not a man.

DONALD HARDING
Oh, Betty. I apologize. I forgot you were here.

ELIZABETH MAHLER
It's all right. I'm married. And I have three boys.

DONALD HARDING
That's right, so you know what I'm talking about. Say,
isn't your eldest in Reggie Sawyer's class?

ELIZABETH MAHLER
Carl? Yes. And the next, Linden, is in Sally's.

DONALD HARDING

Tell us. Carl tell you anything about Reggie? I mean, there's a helluva lot more sex going on in the high school than we adults know about, isn't that right?

ELIZABETH MAHLER

I haven't heard any talk about Reggie.

DONALD HARDING

Who else? Who *does* Carl hear about? You see, Herb? These're the people to talk to. It's going to be somebody in the high school. It stands to reason. And somebody mentally unstable. You know, with a dominant sex drive. What d'ya think, Jack? Have you been checking out the kids in the high school?

DETECTIVE HARRIS

We're working on it. We can't get it done overnight.

DONALD HARDING

No, and we don't expect you to. But have you checked out Reggie Sawyer?

DETECTIVE HARRIS

No, sir. Not yet.

DONALD HARDING

Did you know he used to play with Sally Anders back in first grade?

DETECTIVE HARRIS

No, sir. We didn't have that information.

DONALD HARDING

Well, that's my advice to you. Check out the Sawyer kid. But don't say who gave you the tip.

Monday May 18

OFFICE OF THE FIRST SELECTMAN (Special meeting: 10:30 A.M.) PRESENT: First Selectman Frank Folger; Second Selectman Sam Bowles; Health Officer Dr. Elizabeth Allen; Fire Marshal Ken Davidge; Real-estate developer Steve Polinski.

FIRST SELECTMAN FOLGER
I guess we know why we're here. Steve wanted this meeting. And to tell the truth, I do too. We've got a problem, as I guess you know. Steve, why don't you tell it?

STEVE POLINSKI
Well, it's just this. It's been getting around about Clyde Worth living in my building and I'm starting to feel some heat. I mean, some of my tenants are coming up to me and saying, "How come you're letting Clyde Worth live rent-free? How come I'm paying rent and he isn't?"

SELECTMAN BOWLES
Why don't you tell them they're getting a little more service than Clyde is? Electricity, hot and cold running water.

STEVE POLINSKI
All right, they got no right to complain. Except it does look funny to them, Clyde getting a place out of the kindness of my heart.

SELECTMAN BOWLES
That's the real complaint. They didn't know you had a kind heart.

STEVE POLINSKI
You don't make me mad, Sam. So my rents are high. I charge what the market will bear. That's my right. Most of the other owners in town have lived here too long. They don't know this is a dog-eat-dog world. Let me tell you, when I came here, I couldn't believe what prime locations were renting for. This town was asleep. The turnpike was in, Yale professors were renting houses, turning this into a bedroom town for New Havenites instead of a place full of farmers and fishermen. You landowners here were fifty years behind the times. So I was the one who had to wake you up, let you know what a gold mine this town is, let you know what you can charge for rent for shops on the Green, let you know what to charge for land around here for someone wanting to build a house. So I'm not trying to win a popularity contest. So property values have gone way up all the last reassessments? That's not my doing. They'd have gone up if I'd never seen this place. I'm only charging fair market value.

If my tenants don't like what it costs for a store front on the Green, let them go rent a store somewhere else. I don't twist anybody's arm.

SELECTMAN BOWLES
Lovable Steve.

STEVE POLINSKI
You're one of those who don't want to see this town change. You were born here and you don't want a single new house to go up. It might spoil the view.

FIRST SELECTMAN FOLGER
Oh, hell, we know the town's gonna change. Can't help that. What we want is for the town not to change too fast. We gotta absorb the change in order to keep the town's character. If you're not liked in town, Steve, it's not because the town is growing, it's because you don't care about the town's *character*. All you want to do is milk the town for everything you can get. And when you've got all you can, you'll move out. We know about the property you've got up in New Hampshire.

STEVE POLINSKI
So yell all you want. Everything I do is legal. Everything has to go through Planning and Zoning. You don't like what I do, complain to them.

FIRST SELECTMAN FOLGER
They can't stop you. As you say, it's all legal.

STEVE POLINSKI
Then get the town to change the zoning laws.

DOCTOR ALLEN
I have a patient due at eleven-thirty. If you want anything from me, Frank, I think we should get at it.

FIRST SELECTMAN FOLGER
You're right, Doctor. My apologies. What we're here to
discuss is what to do about Clyde Worth.

DOCTOR ALLEN
You want him back in the mental hospital?

FIRST SELECTMAN FOLGER
Oh, no. Nothing like that. He doesn't belong in any
mental hospital.

DOCTOR ALLEN
Because, if you do, somebody else is going to have to
put him there. I had to do it the last time and he felt I
tricked him. I don't want to do that to him again or I'll
lose his trust altogether.

FIRST SELECTMAN FOLGER
No, no. We aren't planning to put him away. There's
nothing wrong with him. They released him, didn't they?
Clyde doesn't have anything to fear about that.

DOCTOR ALLEN
Then what *is* this meeting about?

FIRST SELECTMAN FOLGER
It's what to do about Clyde.

DOCTOR ALLEN
What's the problem?

FIRST SELECTMAN FOLGER
You tell her, Steve.

STEVE POLINSKI
I own this abandoned building—was the Tinker Shop
when old Leslie Hubbard was alive. I picked it up from
his estate. It's on River Street, almost across from the
movie theater—

DOCTOR ALLEN
I know where it is.

134 HillaryHillary Waugh*

STEVE POLINSKI

I've been busy with other projects—haven't made any plans for it yet. I'm going to convert it into shops, with offices on the second floor. The architect's drawing up some designs right now, but it's a while down the road. Meanwhile, it's sitting empty, not doing anybody any good. The wiring's shot, there never was any water. It'd be cheaper to tear it down and build fresh, but I can't do that because of zoning regulations. I've got to utilize the building as is. So, meanwhile, it sits.

DOCTOR ALLEN

I know all that. And you allowed Clyde Worth to live in it.

STEVE POLINSKI

He was just out of the mental hospital with no place to go. It was sitting empty, so I figured, what the hell, if he could use it, okay, so long as he got out when I needed it.

DOCTOR ALLEN

And now you need it? I thought you said the architect hasn't developed his plans yet, you aren't ready to use it?

STEVE POLINSKI

Well, it's not quite that simple.

FIRST SELECTMAN FOLGER

You saw it last week, Dr. Allen. Don't you think it's a health hazard?

DOCTOR ALLEN
I think it's a fire hazard, but that's for Ken to say. I don't know that it's a health hazard.

STEVE POLINSKI
With all the newspapers, and the smell, and the way he lives?

DOCTOR ALLEN
What do you want from me, Steve?

STEVE POLINSKI
I hadn't been paying attention. I just left him alone. I didn't go check on him. But with all the complaints—

DOCTOR ALLEN
About the way he was living?

STEVE POLINSKI
Well, the talk against him. I don't mean that people really think he had anything to do with what happened to Sally Anders. He's not the type. But all of a sudden, people are worried about him—about what a guy like him *might* do. You know, a guy who's dotty, who collects cats, who lives in a pigsty and doesn't care? After all, it's my building. I'm responsible if the place catches on fire. What if the building burns down and he's in it?

DOCTOR ALLEN

Ken, what's your thinking about this? You're the fire marshal.

FIRE MARSHAL DAVIDGE

I think Steve's right. We've got a dangerous situation here.

DOCTOR ALLEN

Then it's up to you to say so, isn't it? What do you need me here for?

FIRST SELECTMAN FOLGER

Well, Steve and Ken and I were thinking you might be able to say something to him. You're somebody he listens to.

DOCTOR ALLEN

Meaning you want Clyde out of there.

STEVE POLINSKI

That's right. I've been turning my back, figuring he's not hurting anybody. But when I start getting complaints, I gotta pay attention. I was trying to do a good deed, but you know the old saying, "No good deed goes unpunished."

DOCTOR ALLEN

And you want to lay the onus on me?

FIRST SELECTMAN FOLGER
Well, we thought you could make him understand the necessity better.

SELECTMAN BOWLES
So where does Clyde go if you turn him out?

STEVE POLINSKI
Well, hell, that's his business. Where'd he have gone if I hadn't given him the use of the building?

FIRST SELECTMAN FOLGER
I think the point here is that Steve wants Clyde out and we want to do it the easiest way.

SELECTMAN BOWLES
He wants him out because of what happened to the Anders girl?

STEVE POLINSKI
You don't understand. That's not my thinking. I don't think he did anything. But I'm getting complaints. It's come out now the way he's been living. People used not to pay him any attention. Now they're looking at him and deciding he's more dangerous than they thought. Him and all those cats and the stacks of newspapers, and using candles to see his way around.

FIRST SELECTMAN FOLGER
The point is, he's created a dangerous situation. It's dangerous healthwise and firewise. You get a fire in that building, half a dozen other buildings would go up with it. We can't turn our backs on that kind of thing.

SELECTMAN BOWLES
You've been turning your backs on it for almost two years. None of you paid the slightest attention to Clyde and how he lived. Now, all of a sudden, it's a dangerous situation. Because of what happened to the Anders girl. He didn't have anything to do with it, by your own admission, but now he's dangerous and has got to be dispossessed.

FIRST SELECTMAN FOLGER
No. He's got to be dispossessed because Steve wants him out of there. It's Steve's property. Steve's got the right.

SELECTMAN BOWLES
So let Steve tell Clyde to get out. Why the hell is this involving the first selectman, the second selectman, the health official and the fire marshal? What's the matter, Steve? You want us to do your dirty work for you?

STEVE POLINSKI
I'm thinking about the guy.

SELECTMAN BOWLES

So am I.

STEVE POLINSKI

He's got to go. I've done my job. I've supported him for two years. Now I want my property back.

SELECTMAN BOWLES

Now you think he's dangerous. Now you think he might have murdered Sally Anders.

STEVE POLINSKI

Hell, no. Nobody believes that. It was probably Reggie Sawyer.

SECOND SELECTMAN

Reggie Sawyer? The principal of Dudley Bishop Elementary School?

FIRST SELECTMAN FOLGER

Not him, his son.

SELECTMAN BOWLES

Young Reggie? The football player?

                    STEVE POLINSKI
You hadn't heard?

                    SELECTMAN BOWLES
     Heard what?

                    STEVE POLINSKI
     Nobody knows where he was that night. Not his folks,
not his friends. And *he* won't say.

                    SELECTMAN BOWLES
     Is this for real? You suspect *him*?

                    FIRST SELECTMAN FOLGER
     There's no evidence. We aren't saying he was involved,
but the police are making inquiries. And it's suspicious.

                    SELECTMAN BOWLES
     Why? Because he doesn't have an alibi?

                    FIRST SELECTMAN FOLGER
     That's one reason.

                    SELECTMAN BOWLES
     You've gotta have more than that. I'll lay odds half the
kids in his class don't have an alibi for that night.

STEVE POLINSKI
But they aren't Reggie Sawyer!

SELECTMAN BOWLES
What's that supposed to mean?

FIRE MARSHAL DAVIDGE
He's the football star. He's president of the senior class.
Girls look up to somebody like that. Remember when we
were in school, playing football? Remember Bill Hawley?
You were a guard and I was a tackle, but he was the
quarterback. Remember how all the girls looked up to him,
especially girls a class behind? And remember when he got
the wind knocked out of him in the game against Clinton
Center and they carried him off the field on a stretcher?
Remember how the girls were shrieking and tearing their
hair? And you told me there was no glory, playing football,
if you weren't in the backfield? You said they could carry *us*
off the field dead, and the girls wouldn't even notice.

SELECTMAN BOWLES
But Bill was *white*. Reggie's black.

FIRST SELECTMAN
That's why the police are interested in him and what he
was doing that night.

SELECTMAN BOWLES
He wouldn't even *know* Sally Anders, let alone where she
was baby-sitting that night. That doesn't make any sense.

FIRE MARSHAL DAVIDGE
He *does* know Sally Anders. He knew her better than you think.

STEVE POLINSKI
They were dating.

SELECTMAN BOWLES
Sally Anders and Reggie Sawyer?

FIRST SELECTMAN FOLGER
It's all over town. He used to play with her when they were kids, living in the same neighborhood. He'd come over to her house back when they were in grammar school. And it didn't stop there. She was sneaking out to go to the movies with him when she was fourteen.

SELECTMAN BOWLES
Sneaking? How could he sneak her to the movies in a town like Crockford?

FIRST SELECTMAN FOLGER
They didn't go to the movies in Crockford. He took her over to Madison.

SELECTMAN BOWLES
How would he get her there? He'd only be fifteen. He wouldn't have a license.

STEVE POLINSKI

Who needs a license? All he'd need was a car. And he had friends. He was a star athlete. Lots of people would lend him a car.

SELECTMAN BOWLES

You got evidence of this?

FIRST SELECTMAN FOLGER

The police have found people in Madison who saw them together.

SELECTMAN BOWLES

And you think he did it? Why?

FIRST SELECTMAN FOLGER

Well, we haven't worked out the details yet. Like I say, we don't have evidence. All we know is he was out in his car that night. His folks don't know where he went and he isn't saying. He as much as told Jack Harris, who questioned him, that it was none of his business. I mean, that's damned fresh for a kid, especially a black kid, to talk to a police detective. Put it all together, that *makes* it Jack's business.

SELECTMAN BOWLES

Yeah, but what about motive? I mean, what the hell have you got except that he used to know Sally Anders and he doesn't have an alibi.

FIRST SELECTMAN FOLGER

There's nothing to go on yet, but what the police suspect is that he was interested in her—interested in doing more than just going to the movies together. And she was drawing the line. I mean, you can be friendly with blacks and be broad-minded and all that, but that's not the same as going to bed with blacks. So, if she was turning him down, and he didn't like being turned down—well, you know what blacks and Hispanics and people like that are like. It's a macho thing. You read it in the papers about three times a week about how some black or Hispanic in New York murders his sweetheart because she gives him the air.

SELECTMAN BOWLES

Yeah, but that's only theory. You don't have a shred of evidence to back it up.

FIRST SELECTMAN FOLGER

And we don't have any other suspects, either. Look at it that way! The way we see it—the way the police see it—Sally Anders was raped and murdered by somebody who knew her and who knew where she was baby-sitting. It was somebody who knew her and wanted her and was determined to have her. And he also knew he'd have to kill her in the bargain to keep from being identified. That indicates it was somebody who'd approached her and who she rejected—flatly rejected! She probably said, "Don't ever come *near* me again." So the police have been looking for someone among her classmates she was connected with for a little while, or who was rushing her and getting the cold shoulder. And they haven't been able to find anybody direct. All they could come up with was this connection with Reggie Sawyer. I admit it's frail, but it's the *only* thing at all. And then, when you figure what was done to her, and look around at her classmates and think, who in that high school is capable of such a thing, you come up with Reggie Sawyer. Not just because he's black, but he's also a star football player who's got offers from half a dozen colleges. And football is a brutal game, the kind of game that attracts people who have an element of brutality in them. You know what I mean? Isn't that right, Doctor Allen?

DOCTOR ALLEN

I'm a GP, not a psychiatrist. I've heard the stories, but I go to the Congregational Church and certainly Reginald Sawyer Senior is one of its most highly regarded members. He not only sings in the choir and handles all the solo work, he's a member of the vestry and serves on a number of committees. And, certainly, he's made Dudley Bishop Elementary School the best elementary school in town.

STEVE POLINSKI

That's the father you're talking about, Doctor. It doesn't necessarily follow, "like father, like son."

DOCTOR ALLEN

I know that. I also know young Reggie, and I *do* think, "like father, like son." But, to tell you the truth, I've dealt with nearly every student in that high school at one time or another, and I can't imagine any of them doing such a thing. So far as I'm concerned, the only support for the stories about him that are going around is that there aren't any stories at all about anyone else.

FIRST SELECTMAN FOLGER
What we're saying, Sam, is that we've got nothing against the kid except that he won't say what he was doing that night. And if he was doing something *less* criminal than rape and murder, you'd figure he'd be eager to tell us. So we're not saying he's guilty, we're just saying there're a lot of questions about him that need answering.

STEVE POLINSKI
That's right. Nobody's saying he's guilty. That's the law in this country, a person's innocent until *proven* guilty, and we don't have a shred of proof against Reggie Sawyer. We can think what we like, but you can't hang a man for what people think. It's not like the Old Country over here.

DOCTOR ALLEN
I'm sorry, but I have to be going. I have a patient coming.

FIRST SELECTMAN FOLGER
I'm sorry, Elizabeth. We got off the track. Look, the reason we got you here was because you know Clyde better than any of the rest of us. He trusts you. He'll do what you tell him.

DOCTOR ALLEN
I don't know how much he trusts me after I put him into the mental institution.

FIRST SELECTMAN FOLGER
Well, he certainly doesn't trust anyone else. The point
is, Steve wants him to vacate the building, and that's
Steve's right. The problem bothering us—me as first
selectman—is how to do this gently. I can have the police
throw him out, of course. But what would that do to
the man? If we can get the job done gently, so that
he can understand why it's necessary—the place is a
fire hazard, a health hazard—he might go without causing
difficulties.

DOCTOR ALLEN
And you'd rather have *me* tell him it's a health hazard
than have Ken tell him it's a fire hazard?

FIRST SELECTMAN FOLGER
You're more persuasive than Ken.

DOCTOR ALLEN
Well, I can certainly speak to him and I believe I can
make him understand that the change is necessary.

SELECTMAN BOWLES
And where does he go once he's been dispossessed?

FIRST SELECTMAN FOLGER
That's up to him.

SELECTMAN BOWLES
We *aren't* our brother's keeper?

FIRST SELECTMAN FOLGER
Well, hell, Sam, what do you think we're supposed to do as selectmen, find homes for everybody? That's what real-estate agents are for.

SELECTMAN BOWLES
He has no money. Come on!

STEVE POLINSKI
Look, I want him *out*. The rest is up to him.

SELECTMAN BOWLES
Up to him, huh? Where does he go?

FIRE MARSHAL DAVIDGE
How about welfare? We've got a welfare agency. Turn him over to Dot Lemon.

FIRST SELECTMAN FOLGER
Dot can only give out money—after somebody qualifies. She doesn't find people a place to sleep.

FIRE MARSHAL DAVIDGE
Maybe he can sleep in the Good Will bin again.

SELECTMAN BOWLES
That's not funny, Ken. I'm telling you, this is a serious problem. You can't just turn him into the streets. There's no telling what he might do. He might attack the lot of us.

FIRST SELECTMAN FOLGER
Oh come on, Sam. Stop dramatizing. Clyde won't do anything. He's harmless.

SELECTMAN BOWLES
Listen to me. People like him are harmless as long as they can get along. They don't need much. They can live on almost nothing. But if you take *everything* away, if you push them to the wall and leave them with nothing, that's when the mildest, most harmless person in the world can go berserk. Are *you* willing, Doctor Allen, to guarantee that if this one thing in life he's got, his candlelit, newspaper-stacked home full of his beloved cats, is taken away, that Clyde Worth will remain peaceful and harmless and forgiving? Can you guarantee that he won't crack and run amuck?

DOCTOR ALLEN
No. I can't guarantee that.

SELECTMAN BOWLES

Listen to me, all of you. You can't deprive Clyde of *everything*. You have to give him something. If not, you can't let him run around loose. If he can't look after himself, he's got to be looked after.

DOCTOR ALLEN

Sam's right. Clyde can't look after himself and he has no place to go.

FIRST SELECTMAN FOLGER

Except back to the mental hospital.

SELECTMAN BOWLES

At least there he can be cared for.

STEVE POLINSKI

That would solve a lot of problems. He's been more of a one than you know.

FIRE MARSHAL DAVIDGE

At least the townspeople would stop worrying about him.

FIRST SELECTMAN FOLGER

Elizabeth, do you think you can persuade him?

DOCTOR ALLEN

I might be able to get him to agree to go there for tests. Once there, he can be committed.

FIRST SELECTMAN FOLGER

That would be great. He'd be comfortable. We'd all be comfortable. Elizabeth, would you see what you can do?

DOCTOR ALLEN

I might be able to persuade him to go willingly, if he'll trust me after the last time. But he'll never trust me again.

Thursday May 21

It was Jane Anders who made the discovery. But let her tell you about it.

JANE ANDERS

You know, I try to bring up my children—tried to, that is—bring up my children right. There isn't any Sally anymore. They say you get used to it, but I can't. I haven't been much good for anything or anybody since it happened. It's two weeks now. Two weeks ago today. They say time heals. I don't know who says that. Whoever did, didn't lose a daughter. My father died when I was thirty-two. I could handle that. He was sixty-three and had been bedridden for three years. People told me I should be glad he was free of the bed and the pain, but still I wept. Because, even pale and hurting, with that awful pain in his eyes, he was alive. He was still my father. And when he was gone, I missed him. I'll always miss him. I don't know where he is now. I only know he's gone. I'll never see him again. Maybe that's selfish. Cally Baker—she's my cousin—told me I had no right to weep.

She was there, helping with the arrangements, and she doesn't know the meaning of the word *sympathy*. "You've got no business weeping," she told me. "Don't you have any idea what he was going through?" Cally's all in favor of euthanasia. "When are we going to outgrow these old-fashioned beliefs," she says, "that we're doing people a favor keeping them alive, that *any* life is better than *no* life." She claims God invented Death for a purpose and we persist in trying to thwart that purpose. That's funny, coming from her. She doesn't believe in God. She never has.

But let's not talk about my father. I wept for him— Cally told me I was feeling sorry for myself instead of feeling glad for him. But time healed the wound. I was able to turn toward the future and face life, a life without my father in it. It wouldn't be as good a life, but it was still a life I could smile in and be glad in.

It's not the same this time.

Please don't tell me that time heals *all* wounds. It will never heal this one. Friends try to comfort me by saying I will learn to smile again, even laugh. Don't believe them. You don't know the depression! Nobody does! Where have I failed? What have I done wrong that this could have happened to her? I don't mean, where have I sinned that this should be my punishment. I'm not thinking of that. We all fail. I fail daily, fail miserably. It's not that. It's Sally! What did I teach her, or not teach her, or fail her in some way, that brought her to this horrible end? God! How *can* you? Do what You *want* to me! She didn't deserve it! I'd've died in her stead, if I could. I'm old and bedraggled and used up. I'm no use to Jim. We don't get along. It's probably my fault we don't get along, that he avoids me—all the while pretending he isn't. Sally avoided me too. And Christopher. And all I was trying to do was keep a home, make my husband happy, raise my children right, and make our family something of which the community could be proud! Is that bad? Is that why God should punish me? Is that why Sally should die?

All right, I'm sorry. I didn't mean to talk about Sally. But she's always in the forefront of my mind. Her face is constantly before me and I wonder what I did wrong. I got over my father's death. I'm sure I'll get over my mother's when the time comes—but, please, God, not too soon. Not after this. But for anyone to tell me that I'll smile again after Sally's death, that I'll get over it, that's asking too much. There are some wounds Time can't ever heal!

But I have to tell about the thing that happened—with Christopher. He's thirteen, you understand. And he's lost his sister. He grieves too. It's been two weeks, but the pain hasn't lessened. Not for any of us. He mopes. He doesn't play with his friends anymore. He goes to school and comes home and pretends to busy himself with his schoolbooks and homework. And Jim. We didn't talk much before; now we hardly talk at all. The three of us are pretending this is a household. Jim doesn't say so, but I think his work is suffering. It's two weeks now, but the pain doesn't lessen; it's getting worse. We're coming down to earth now, getting over the numbing shock and beginning to face the terrible reality that Sally isn't going to come home again, that there's an empty bedroom off the upstairs bath with the bed left just the way she made it before she went to school that last day. It's not the neatest bed in the world, not one I'd want to show people and say, "This is how she left her room." She didn't have my desire for neatness. She hadn't yet come to realize that a woman's house is her badge of merit. I tried to instill it in her, make her comprehend, but it would have taken more time. She'd have realized it if there'd been more time.

I've tried my best to keep the household going, busied myself with routine. My mind wanders, but I've tried, ever since it happened, to keep my hands busy. I've pretended that the look of the house is as important now as it was before.

That's what this is all about. The children—Sally and Christopher. Right from the beginning I made them keep their rooms tidy, make their beds, pick up their toys and things, be neat. Sally was always perfunctory: "Yes, Mother," and try to make the bedspread hide the wrinkles underneath. Christopher was hopeless. Oh, he made his bed, but you'd think an elephant had slept in it. And the rest? Things were always lying around. "Oh, I forgot," he'd say. That was his password. It defines him.

Well, once a week, I'd make their beds—give them clean sheets. Mondays. I gave them a day off. And the thing I'd do, which would never occur to them, was to turn their mattresses over. They'd keep the same side up for a million years, never give their mattress an airing.

And that's how I discovered, a year ago, a salacious magazine hidden under Chris's mattress. I don't mean *Playboy*, or even *Hustler*. This was a cheap pulp thing, with black-and-white pictures of the most disgraceful exhibitions of men and women together in the most degrading poses.

I showed it to Jim. I thought the boy was debauched. I couldn't imagine how he got hold of such a thing, let alone why he'd be interested. Chris had always seemed so straight. I expected Jim to flip!

Instead, he laughed. He didn't take it seriously. I said I feared it would lead to masturbation and I'd heard that kind of thing could affect a person's mind.

As for Jim, he said he didn't know if Chris was capable yet. He said he didn't start masturbating till he was fourteen. I was shocked that he'd admit to such a thing. But Jim just said all boys did it, and that it was natural for boys to have an interest in sex and in what girls looked like without their clothes on. And he told me another shocking thing—that it wasn't just when they grew up. He told me when he was six, a playmate, who had a four-year-old sister, used to get the three of them in a closet and have her pull down her pants. She'd giggle and oblige, but didn't know why it entertained them. What Jim wanted me to believe was that boys like that sort of thing at *any* age.

Well, I was shocked. I said I'd show Chris what I'd found and shame him. Jim advised me not to. He said it wouldn't change anything. All Chris would do would be to find a better hiding place. He thought my best move would be to replace the magazine and pretend I never knew about it.

I did. I don't know why, except that I realized I don't have the faintest idea what men are all about. I only knew that Jim had never acted like a sexual maniac with me and if he'd done these things, like letting a four-year-old girl pull down her pants when he was only six, and he'd masturbated and looked at pornographic magazines, and he'd grown up to be respectable and the kind of man a girl like me could fall in love with—and I did fall in love with him—maybe this salacious magazine I found under Chris's mattress wouldn't do him all that much harm. And Jim had said I couldn't stop him anyway. I'd just drive him into hiding. So I replaced the magazine and pretended I didn't know anything about it.

And from time to time there'd be other things under the mattress that Chris didn't want us knowing about—other magazines, sometimes nude pictures which would show more than I'd show to my own husband. But I didn't bother Jim about them anymore. I left them where they were and pretended I didn't know about them.

Until last Monday. When I turned the mattress over on Monday, what I found under there was a packet of—well, the word is getting to be commonplace now, though I've never used it before—condoms.

That was more than I could handle. Chris is only thirteen. I had to show it to Jim.

I handed it to him and told him where I found it after finishing the dinner dishes, when Chris was doing homework and Jim was poring over a tome on the history of Greece. He thinks ancient Greece was when all was right with the world. Or he pretends to. That's all he's done since Sally died. Every evening, till it's time to go to bed. He's hiding from reality, is my guess, pretending nothing happened.

But this woke him up a little. Jim looked very sober. This time, even he was shook up. He studied the packet, stood up, put it in his pocket, and said he'd talk to Chris—alone. He stressed the *alone*. That was fine with me. I don't want to know about all the things men do.

Thursday May 21

JIM ANDERS

I don't know what I was thinking when I went up to Chris's room with that packet in my pocket. I don't know that I've been thinking much at all the past couple of weeks. I don't really know what I've been doing except walking through the days like an automaton, isolating myself. I've been feeling sorry for myself, I expect. That's how the psychiatrists would figure it. I can't keep from picturing the days that will never be—Sally's graduation next year, Sally getting accepted at Brown, her ambition, and I'm sure she would have made it. Mostly, I see me walking her down the aisle of St. Bartholomew's Church, she in her wedding gown, scared to death, with me squeezing the hand she's got through my arm, giving her me to lean on one last time. And it's fatal to think about things like that.

But that packet of condoms woke me up that Sally wasn't the only child in our family, that Christopher was equally dear and I couldn't let him drift and drown out of

158

my grief for the one I'd lost. What the hell was he up to? That's what I couldn't understand.

His door was open off the top of the stairs and he was bending over his math. Kids are resilient. He was back almost to normal already. He was over at his friend Pete Herly's this afternoon.

"Hi," he grunted, giving me a strange look at my unexpected intrusion. It made me realize how long it's been since he's come to me for help with his homework. I felt as if I didn't really know him any longer. Especially with what I was holding in my pocket.

I took out the packet and dropped it on his desk. "Where'd you get this, Chris?"

He blanched and looked up. "Where'd you find that?"

"I'm asking you where you got it."

He didn't pretend innocence. "I got it from a friend."

"Why? What are you doing with it?"

"Nothing."

"People don't buy those things for 'nothing,' Chris. I'm asking you, what are you doing with it?"

"I said, I'm keeping it for a friend."

"Why can't the friend keep it for himself?"

"Because . . . because . . . There are reasons."

"Are you using those things? Are you capable? Have you—"

He came to his feet. "What're you talking about? Of course not. How could you believe I'd have anything to do with—that crap. Sex is for the birds. What about AIDS?" His voice grew shrill. "Don't you know about AIDS?"

I closed the door to keep Jane from hearing. I came back, trying to think how to handle the situation. Parents are supposed to be so smart, and they're so dumb. "Look," I said, and wanted to put a caring hand on his shoulder, but sensed he'd feel I was condescending, "I care about you. Believe it or not, I care about you."

"Sure you do. The only time you care about me is when you poke through my things and find something like that. The rest of the time, you don't even know I live here."

"Most of the time," I said, "I honor your right to privacy and to mind your own business. That's because I respect you and the way you conduct yourself. If I appear to be 'caring' all of a sudden, it's because I've found something that makes me suspect I've been wrong, that I *can't* respect the way you conduct yourself. And your excuse for why this packet was found in your possession makes me respect you even less."

"I said it wasn't mine! I said I wouldn't be caught dead!" His voice was aggressive and shrill, but there were tears behind his eyes and I realized suddenly how young he was, how sensitive, and how my impugning him had hurt. He didn't want to cry. He hadn't cried over Sally, though I'd seen those same hidden tears. He was trying so hard to be a man, and it's so difficult when you're still a boy. I remembered myself in those years.

"Look," I said, "I'm not accusing you. I'm sure you're not into anything like that. I'm only wondering what you're doing with something like this. Who gave it to you to keep? Who do you know who wants you to keep such a thing for him? Who wants to give you that burden? What are they doing it for?"

"Nobody gave it to me," he fought back. The tears were starting to show. "Why don't you leave me alone?"

"Somebody must have given it to you. You couldn't have bought them."

"I found them," he exclaimed. "If you must know, I *found* them!"

"You found them? Where?"

"It's none of your business! Leave me alone!"

His desperation made me realize how important it was that he tell me. "Chris," I said, "I want to know where these came from. I want to know where you found them."

Tears started down his cheeks and he had to wipe them away with his hand. "It's nobody's business where I found them," he answered. "I just found them, that's all."

"I want to know where, Chris."

"No you don't. Throw them away." He snatched up the packet and tried to put it in the wastebasket.

I took his wrist. "No, Chris. Problems don't go away that easily. There's something about where you found them that's bothering you. I want to know why. I want to know where you found them that makes you feel so ashamed to say."

"They aren't mine, I tell you. They don't have anything to do with me." The tears were flowing down both cheeks now and he no longer tried to wipe them away. There was a sob in his voice as well. The little boy in him was defeating the man.

"They have to do with somebody close to you, Chris. Who is it? Where did you find them?"

Now he sobbed. "In Sally's drawer."

I don't know if anything ever hit me harder. I don't know why a father thinks any other girl in the world is capable of any kind of activity but not his own daughter. Not until this moment had the thought occurred to me that Sally might have been sexually active. I view myself as broad-minded. I'm up to date enough not to be shocked by our modern mores. Had Sally been dating heavily, going steady with some boy, I wouldn't have been surprised if she'd been having sex. In fact, I might have been surprised if she weren't.

But Sally had had no special beau. Her best friends were girls. She dated, but the dates weren't that often and the boys had seemed more friends than lovers. That's why a packet of condoms in her drawer came as such a shock. Was she into—not just sex—but casual sex? She'd seemed so much the 4-H type girl, interested in the world at large, in friends and activities, with sex lying far down the road of her future. What depths had there been in my daughter that I hadn't suspected?

Chris could read the shock in my face. "So now you know," he said, and I realized from the bitterness of his tone the shock it had been to him as well. And he'd hidden the condoms to protect her.

I had to say something. "How did you find them?" I

asked, trying to sound normally curious. I hoped he wasn't
a sneak who made a practice of probing his sister's drawers.

"Mom said, before she put away Sally's things, that if
there was anything of hers I wanted, I could have it." He
rubbed away the tears on his cheeks and his voice was
firmer. He was over the worst of it and was trying to
explain. "I thought I'd like the silver Tiffany pen you gave
her for her sixteenth birthday. Mom said I could have it.
It wasn't on her dresser. I didn't know where she kept it.
I went through her drawers. She had it in the little bag it
came in, in the box it came in, with the card it came with,
under all her underwear at the very back of the drawer.
She was keeping it protected. And before I found the pen,
I found that!" He gestured in disgust at the packet. "And I
thought Mom was going to put away all her things and I
didn't want Mom to find *that* when she did, so I took it.
And I hid it. Because I didn't know what to do. I didn't
want Mom or you to find it. I didn't want anybody to ever
find it."

The boy who wanted to be a man was really quite a
man.

I sat down on the bed, all the strength gone out of me.
He said, "Are you going to tell?"

"I have to think about that," I said.

"Then everybody will call her a whore."

"It might help the police find out who killed her."

"They'll call her a whore. They'll say she asked for it."

"You don't care who killed her?"

"I don't know if it matters anymore. That's what she
was, wasn't she? My sister?"

"It doesn't necessarily mean that. You mustn't leap to
conclusions, Chris."

"It's not much of a leap."

"She's still your sister. You hid those condoms to protect her."

"And you found them and you're going to tell, and
everybody's going to spit on her."

I got up from the bed. This time I did put a hand on his

shoulder. "The world isn't black and white," I said. "You can't damn her forever for what you found in her drawer. She's not here to defend herself. There's a vast area between being a virgin and being a prostitute. We don't know what she was doing, or why. We don't even know that *she* wasn't just keeping them for a 'friend.' "

"*I* know," he said. He put his elbows on his desk and dug at his overflowing eyes with his palms.

Friday May 22

REGGIE SAWYER

Crockford sucks.

You grow up in a town. You think it's a nice place to live. You think you've got a lot of friends. You think people like you. And then you find out the whole place sucks. The people suck. They don't like you, they never did. They only pretended to, to make themselves feel noble.

Sure, I knew Sally Anders. I knew who she was. She was a junior. Blond, not bad-looking. I'm not trying to speak ill of the dead, but she wasn't all that great-looking either. She was a nice kid. I remember her best, I suppose, playing Laurie last year in the high school production of *Oklahoma!*, especially the first scene when she's looking out of an upstairs window, fixing her hair and enjoying the morning. That's the picture I have of Sally Anders.

The word's around town that I dated her, that we went together, sneaking over to movies in Madison, that I lusted for her, that I killed her because she wouldn't let

164

me—well, I'm not going to use whitey words like "screw her." There're people in town think I killed her, that I knew she was baby-sitting at the Parkers' that night—May the seventh—and I went there and raped her, and then murdered her so she couldn't tell on me.

Nobody says that to my face. Nobody accuses me of anything, they just look at me like I'm a born rapist-killer. Because I've got black skin.

They say I spent a couple of afternoons playing with her at her house on State Street back in the first grade. I'd forgotten about that. First grade was a long time ago. I remember it a little now—playing with a girl. But I couldn't've told you who it was. I guess it must've been Sally because back when I was in first grade, when my folks moved into town because my father was made assistant principal at the high school under Carter MacLaine, whom he'd been assistant to in a high school in New Haven, we did live for a couple of years on State Street, not too far from the Anders. And I have a vague recollection of a little blond girl, and her folks, and what their yard was like. And I do kind of remember wrestling with her and teasing her and enjoying it. What else can you do with a girl? It wasn't quite like being with a boy. That's why I remember it. Because it was different. And in a way it was kind of fun. I didn't too much mind that she wasn't a boy and that we couldn't do what I did with the boys I played with on the sidewalks and streets in New Haven. I mean, girls aren't the same as boys. But I was new in town and I didn't know any boys. I didn't know any kids on State Street to play with. And once, or maybe twice, these people had me over to play with their little girl. And they fed us milk and cookies. I remember especially the cookies. I hadn't had cookies before, not that good. I still remember the cookies.

But we moved. My folks, that is. Dad got his job changed. When they built the new Dudley Bishop Elementary School, he was made principal and he got us a home on North Hill Road. That's where we live now. And I never saw Sally Anders again, until high school. In fact,

I didn't even know her name, or remember I'd ever seen her before, until what happened to her two weeks ago and people started saying she was the girl I spent one or two afternoons with when we were starting grammar school.

Now it's a big deal. Now there're people claiming we've been seeing each other right along. People are saying we dated, that we sneaked around together. I swear, I never knew the Sally Anders I saw in the school play was the same girl whose folks had me come over and play with— until she was killed. I knew who she was in high school, because of her being in that show last year, but I swear, I never spoke a word to her.

So why do people think I raped and killed her? Why do people think I lusted? Why do the stories make no sense if you stop to think? It's because I'm black. I've got black skin in a white community.

I thought this was a great town. I loved this town. I loved the people. I thought this was one place where there was no black prejudice. I mean, I never really encountered black prejudice. Where I lived in New Haven, it was all black. I didn't see any whites except passing through, like strangers. But I didn't think anything of it. I was too young. I was five years old when my dad got the job here as assistant principal.

Then, all of a sudden, everybody was white—almost everybody. There're a few blacks and Hispanics in town, but you somehow don't notice them. There aren't enough of them, and they act like everybody else, so you don't notice any difference. Like me playing with Sally Anders in first grade. All I noticed about her was that she was a girl, and I wasn't much used to girls. What color her skin was made no impression.

Of course, I didn't grow to where I am now without noticing the difference, without knowing I was different. Dad brought his old mother in to live with us. She was a laundress in New Haven, went around to white people's houses in the Depression, in the days before washing machines, and for two dollars a day—she had to walk or pay her own carfare—she'd wash the clothes in a tub by hand, with the old washboard which I don't think anybody in my school has ever seen except me, and hang out the clothes on the line, and iron everything in the late afternoon and fold it all and find her way home again. That was before I remember very much, but I have that picture because she took me with her a couple of times when Dad was very young and teaching in a black school, and my mother was picking up spare money working in a bakery.

Gramma was a large woman with very flat feet that hurt. She lived with us, retired like, until I was twelve, which was when she died. Dad told her when he brought her here that she'd done for him, now it was his turn to do for her, and she was never going to wash another shirt or iron another sheet. But Dad didn't know Gramma. She wouldn't sit and watch television the way he wanted her to, she did washing and ironing for us. You couldn't stop her. "If you stop moving, you die," she told me. "If I sat and watched television, I'd go in a week. If you aren't useful to the world, you don't belong in it."

And she washed and ironed, no matter how Dad scolded. But she did use the washing machine. She did deign to use that.

But what I learned about black and white was from her. Not from my father. He was *accepted* in this town. He came in as assistant principal in the high school—I suppose they'd call it "enlightenment"—and they turned over the new grammar school to him and praised him for the way he ran it. And he was soloist in the church choir, and he was revered for his voice—he'd never had lessons, but what a gorgeous voice. I'd almost cry listening to that voice up behind me in church on Sundays. But I was a football star and president of the class, and supposed to set a standard for the others! I wasn't supposed to cry.

And he was on the Board of Deacons and other things, and people listened when he spoke. And I was proud. To have him for a father. I wanted to try to be as good a man as he was.

It was Gramma who told me about prejudice. I'd never seen it firsthand. I didn't know what it was. She'd lived

most of her life in the North—in New Haven, but her
folks came from the South and she'd been brought up
with it. She told me things it took me a long time to
understand—like, where we sit ourselves on a bus around
here doesn't matter. But down there, when she was there,
it was "black in the back." It took a while to know what
she was talking about. But I came to understand—in my
brain at least—what she understood from the gut.

She was *black*. Blacker than I. I mean, *real* black. And
she told me it was a blessing. Because, down South, there
wasn't any question what she was or where she belonged.
Then she told me about difference in blackness, how the
blacks with whiter skins would snoot the ones with darker
skins. There was a caste system among blacks. The whiter
you are, the better. And she talked about crossing the
color line—when your skin's so white you can be mistaken
for a white, and then you *pretend* you're white and
have no truck with blacks anymore. Like some black entertainers, she told me. Some, when they got accepted
by "white folk"—that was what she called everybody,
including Dad's and Mom's friends in town, who'd come
for dinner and stuff—she told me, some would use
that wedge to try to help others get accepted. But
there were some black entertainers, but she wouldn't
tell me their names, who, when they crossed the barrier,
turned their backs and got snootier than any of the
whites.

And she told me about a cousin who was a major in the
army in World War II, and how, when he got transferred
and drove from Georgia to the West Coast, there was a
stretch of three days where a black man couldn't get a
lodging for the night. If he hadn't had friends along the
route, he couldn't have done it. She told me one time he
was so hungry he went into a café and ordered breakfast
and the proprietor told him they didn't serve Negroes. He
was in uniform and he was very light-skinned and he
looked at the guy and said, "Do I look like a *Negro*?" and
the guy backed off and served him. Her cousin told her,
"I hated to have to do that, but I was desperate." She had

other stories, but I remember that one because I kept thinking, "Where did he go to the bathroom?"

I thought it was make-believe, the world that my Gramma told me about. I thought it was on the other side of the earth.

And now I find I've been wrong. I find my dear, dead Gramma knew more about the world than I ever will. I didn't comprehend what she told me back then. But I was polite—I didn't pooh-pooh her to her face—nobody could do that. She had the wisdom, the patience, and the understanding of a saint. I used to think, when she told me about going to the back of the bus in Alabama, "Why don't you say, 'I have a right!' " But I wouldn't say that to her. She wasn't a fighter, a rebel. She was an accepter.

Well, I'm a fighter. I listened to these stories she'd tell me, and I'd look around and say, smugly, "That might have happened there, or back in your day. But this is today. And this is Crockford. This is the new world and you're out of date. Look at my father—he's no 'token' black, brought in to make the community look good. He's a leader in this town, respected and revered. And look at me. I'm one of four or five black students in the high school, and look what I've achieved. And you can't say it's just because I'm a good football player and I've been offered scholarships at half a dozen colleges—that they only care about my athletic ability. I'm also president of the senior class! That ought to prove there's no racism in Crockford."

And now I've discovered I've been wrong. My father's been wrong. We think we're being accepted for what we are. And it turns out we're wrong. Something goes awry in the town. A pretty girl gets senselessly murdered, and, without any evidence, where do the fingers point? To the boy in the class who's got black skin.

The cops want to know what I was doing that night. It's not their business, unless they want to know what *every* male student in Crockford High was doing that night. But they don't ask all the others. They come down on me!

And I say, "The hell with them. Ask the boys who

knew her." But the finger's pointed at me! Because I'm black.

And I suddenly realize that racism isn't something that happens "over there," or "down in Alabama," or in some other town. It's here in this town, and I've been living with it and not realizing it, until now. I'm not president of the class because I'm competent and dedicated and sincere, it's because it'll look good in the school annals—Reggie Sawyer (black) was president of the class in 19——. The Board of Education can pat itself on the back for that one.

And my father, principal of one of the grammar schools, bulwark of the church? From everywhere people can point: "Look at Crockford! Look what a black bastard can achieve in Crockford! Who can call Crockford racist?"

The hell with the town. The hell with its sanctimonious piety. I don't even care who the hell killed Sally Anders. She's a symbol of the *stink* of this town. Whatever happened, she didn't deserve it, but that's the town's fault.

As for me, I'm getting out. I'm mailing the high school my resignation as president of the senior class. I won't be there for graduation. They can send the diploma to "Address Unknown" or throw it in a trash barrel for all I give a damn. I hate this sucking town. I don't know where I'm going, but it's going to be so far away I'll forget I ever lived here. Maybe I'll give my folks an address when I decide what I'm going to do with my life. Maybe I'll tell them what I was really doing that night, in case the town gets after them too! Right now, I curse the day we came here. Why did my father and mother have to be black?

Monday May 25

POLICE COMMISSION MEETING—EXECUTIVE SES-
SION (8:30 P.M.) PRESENT: Hugh McCormick (Chairman);
Donald Harding; Charles Parker; Chief Herbert Hickey;
Patrolwoman Elizabeth Mahler (Recording Secretary).

HUGH McCORMICK
As if Emily Daitch doesn't give me a hard enough time
about these executive-session meetings, I'm getting calls
from the publishers of the New Haven papers. The publishers! John McIntyre, owner of the *Journal*, was bugging
me less than an hour ago, right in the middle of supper,
about not letting his reporters attend these sessions. He
was trying to claim freedom of information rights, claiming we're illegal.

CHARLES PARKER
What'd you tell him?

171

HUGH McCORMICK

I told him to talk to our town counsel.

DONALD HARDING

That FOI act makes it harder and harder to have a frank discussion about anything. You always have to worry about the public finding out what you said. It's damned inhibiting, let me tell you. Especially when you have to do job evaluations on people, like me.

HUGH McCORMICK

I don't know why they can't go where the action is. Did you see the size of the truck Steve Polinski needed to empty out the Tinker Shop after they got rid of Clyde and his cats? Any enterprising newspaper would've had a photographer as well as a reporter on hand. You'd need a picture to believe how much junk was in that place. But nobody covered it. Even Emily wasn't there.

DONALD HARDING

Reporters don't want to cover news, they want to cover dirt.

CHARLES PARKER

What'd they do with Clyde? I missed all that.

HUGH McCORMICK

He's back in the mental ward. The VA hospital. He was a veteran, I understand.

DONALD HARDING
Clyde Worth was a veteran? You're kidding.

HUGH McCORMICK
Dr. Allen tells me he's got the Purple Heart.

CHARLES PARKER
What happened to all his cats?

CHIEF HICKEY
We had to destroy them. The pet-control officer couldn't find anybody to take them and we can't have thirteen homeless cats roaming around town. That was Frank Folger's decision, and I concur. Of course, we aren't telling Clyde.

CHARLES PARKER
He'll find out pretty damned well quick when he gets out of the mental ward.

HUGH McCORMICK
What about that, Herb? How long before he comes back?

CHIEF HICKEY
Doctor Allen says don't expect him back. She thinks he's there for good.

CHARLES PARKER
Why? Is he maniacal?

CHIEF HICKEY
She says he just sits all day and stares at the wall.
He doesn't talk to anybody—not just not to her, he doesn't
talk to anybody. You spoon-feed him and he eats. You
take him to the john, and he goes. He's docile as a lamb,
no trouble at all, but he's not going to be able to look after
himself any more.

DONALD HARDING
Not that he looked all that much after himself when he
was living in that pigpen with thirteen cats.

CHARLES PARKER
Now I guess we don't have to worry about Clyde picking up any more stray books along the roadside and giving
them to the library.

CHIEF HICKEY
There didn't seem to be much choice, Mr. Parker. I
didn't like getting him recommitted any more than Dr.
Allen did.

DONALD HARDING
I didn't notice anything in the paper about him being
recommitted, and not a word about the pile of junk he left
behind. Never mind news. The press is too goddam busy
trying to find out what we talk about in executive session!

HUGH McCORMICK

Well, getting down to business, one thing we *can* talk about, without worrying about the word leaking out, is that packet of condoms Sally Anders was keeping in her drawer.

DONALD HARDING

Yeah, *that's* all over town. If she'd died a virgin, you couldn't give the information away. Find a packet of condoms in her drawer, and you can't keep it secret.

HUGH McCORMICK

Who the hell spread the word, anyway?

CHARLES PARKER

Not I. All I know is Jim Anders called me Saturday morning, said he had something to show me. He handed me the packet in my study. He didn't even let Pam see it. He didn't know if it was important to the case but he thought he ought to tell me. I said it was evidence and the police ought to see it, it might give a whole new slant to the case. I said I'd have to show it to Herb and go by what he thought.

CHIEF HICKEY

I discussed the matter with Detective Sergeant Dean, since he's in charge of the investigation, and we both agreed it changes everything. It means she might have arranged to meet someone, that maybe the caller wasn't unexpected. It puts a whole new light on the case.

CHARLES PARKER

Except, if she was going to invite some man to *my* house for sex while she's baby-sitting, which, I must say, I don't for one minute believe, why wouldn't she have been carrying the condoms with her?

CHIEF HICKEY

It might have been an extra packet. That's our thinking. The important point is that the condoms show she was sexually active, which is something we hadn't thought before. That's bound to make a difference.

HUGH McCORMICK

So who'd you tell besides Harry Dean and me?

CHIEF HICKEY

I told Harry not to mention it to anyone except the detectives working on the case with him. And I called you, of course. But that's the only people I've told.

HUGH McCORMICK

And, of course, I passed the word to Don when I called this special meeting to discuss the new aspects of the case. But I didn't tell anybody else.

DONALD HARDING

I heard it from Bert Richards before I heard it from you, Hugh. He told me coming out of church yesterday morning. If Bert found out about it, it's a cinch everybody in town would know. That's the kind of gossip Bert loves to spread. I'm probably one of the last to hear about it.

ELIZABETH MAHLER
Chief Hickey told me when he told me about this meeting. But I haven't told anybody, not even my husband.

HUGH McCORMICK
Well, what's done is done. That's the kind of story that's going to come out no matter what you do. And maybe it's a good thing. The more people who know what she was up to, the more chance we might get some fingers pointed in the right direction. Herb, what's your and Harry Dean's thinking on this?

CHIEF HICKEY
Harry and Jack Harris interviewed Mr. and Mrs. Anders Saturday afternoon. They were trying to get a lead on who Sally was seeing, who her boyfriends were, what boys liked her or didn't like her or were jealous of her—things like that. The trouble was, they couldn't help them. They didn't seem to know anything about her private life.

HUGH McCORMICK
Now that's crazy. If boys took her out, they'd know it, wouldn't they? They must have some idea.

DONALD HARDING

Not if she was sneaking over to Madison to the movies with Reggie Sawyer. She tells them she's going out with the girls and sneaks out with the boys. It happens all the time. It doesn't surprise me her folks didn't know what she was up to.

HUGH McCORMICK

Yeah, but that Reggie Sawyer stuff was just rumor.

DONALD HARDING

Where there's smoke, there's fire.

CHIEF HICKEY

We tried to track down those rumors and nobody was a witness. No one was willing to testify they saw Reggie and Sally together, in Madison or anywhere else.

DONALD HARDING

Yeah? Well, I don't know whether you've heard this or not, but I've got it from the grapevine that Reggie Sawyer's left town. He's flown, and his folks don't know where he is. So what do you think of that? That doesn't make him look so innocent?

CHIEF HICKEY

We don't have anything on him.

DONALD HARDING

An innocent man doesn't flee. That's something on him right there.

CHARLES PARKER

He might have been scared. A lot of people were looking his way.

DONALD HARDING

Scared of what, being lynched? We don't do that kind of thing, so what's he got to be scared of? I'm telling you, there's a reason that kid left town, and I think it has to do with his not being able to tell where he was the night Sally got murdered.

CHIEF HICKEY

His folks were in yesterday. They're pretty worried. He was gone Friday night and all day Saturday. He didn't leave a note or take anything with him, and they were afraid he might have been in an accident or something. But they'd called all the hospitals and the morgue in New Haven, but there was no sign of him, or any reports of accidents with a victim unidentified. They were getting frantic. We checked and found he'd cleaned out his bank account, which means he went away on purpose—

DONALD HARDING

That spells guilt to me.

CHIEF HICKEY
Mr. Sawyer called in today, said they'd received a phone
call from him that he's all right, but he said he wasn't
coming back. Mr. Sawyer said Reggie told him, if he wanted
to know why, he'd left a written message. Mr. Sawyer said
he found the message, but he won't turn it over to us.

DONALD PARKER
Well, are you going after the kid?

CHIEF HICKEY
Mr. Sawyer didn't want us to. He said let him be.

DONALD HARDING
And that's that, huh? Since when does Reggie Sawyer
Senior tell the police department what to do?

CHIEF HICKEY
It's not for us to track the kid down if his parents won't
report him missing.

DONALD HARDING
Why the hell not? He's your chief suspect.

CHIEF HICKEY
We don't see it that way. There's not a shred of evidence against him. In fact, that packet of condoms pretty

well puts him in the clear. What we have to do now is find someone Sally Anders was involved with.

DONALD HARDING
One—or a hundred and one.

HUGH McCORMICK
I'll settle for just one. What about that, Herb?

CHIEF HICKEY
So far we haven't been able to get a line on anybody. When I said the Anders didn't know much about her personal life, I don't mean they didn't know *anything*. It wasn't that she never dated, but she didn't date often and didn't have any steady beau that they knew about. The boys who came around were more like friends than lovers.

HUGH McCORMICK
What about her brother, the one who found the condoms? He'd know more about her than her folks.

CHIEF HICKEY
Harry and Jack talked to him too—after they talked to her parents. He's pretty upset about what he found, but he didn't know any more about her sex life than her folks.

CHARLES PARKER
So where do we stand? What's all that mean?

CHIEF HICKEY
Well, the way we interpret it is, the condoms mean she was having sex. The lack of any clues as to who with makes us think she wasn't an easy lay—putting out for any guy who came along. A girl who does that gets a reputation, and we'd have picked it up. We therefore think it may be with just one guy. We think there's a man in her life somewhere. But we don't have the slightest inkling where.

CHARLES PARKER
And you think he raped and killed her?

CHIEF HICKEY
We don't know. If he was having sex with her already, it's hard to see why he'd kill her.

CHARLES PARKER
In other words, those condoms might be a red herring? They might have nothing to do with what happened to her at all?

CHIEF HICKEY
That could be the case. Nevertheless, we certainly want to find out who the man is. Finding that out might answer a lot of other questions.

HUGH McCORMICK
Got anybody in mind?

CHIEF HICKEY
We've got so little to go on it's anybody's guess. But I will say we think it might be an older man.

HUGH McCORMICK
Why that?

CHIEF HICKEY
Because it was so secret. If she had a boyfriend her own age, it seems unlikely none of her friends would know about it.

CHARLES PARKER
And an older man, someone with a position and reputation to uphold, would insist on secrecy!

DONALD HARDING
And might kill her to keep her from exposing him! Hey, I think we've got something here! Now, who the hell—Who knew that girl? What older men was she involved with?

CHIEF HICKEY
We don't have any line on that.

DONALD HARDING

Did you question her parents about that angle? They'd know. You know—she had a special interest in some course at school; talked about what a great teacher somebody was? What groups did she belong to that were headed by an older man? You know, Girl Scouts, or church, or homemakers, or Red Cross, or the *Shoreline News?* Didn't she do a column on high school activities for the *Shoreline News?* I think we're getting somewhere!

CHARLES PARKER

That's right, she did do a column for the *Shoreline News.*

DONALD HARDING

Phil Croft! He's the editor. How about him?

HUGH McCORMICK

Oh, hell, Don, Phil's sixty-three. He's got grandchildren.

DONALD HARDING

What's that supposed to do, rule him out?

CHIEF HICKEY

We don't have any evidence.

DONALD HARDING

God, always evidence! The policeman's mind! Let's use some imagination. I *like* it. It's an older man. She's been having an affair with an older man and he doesn't want the fact to come out.

HUGH McCORMICK

Yes, but Phil Crofts? Him and his "Our town must be made safe again" editorial?

DONALD HARDING

Well, who else? What other older men would she know? You been looking into this, Herb?

CHIEF HICKEY

We haven't had a chance to yet.

DONALD HARDING

How about her school? What about her teachers?

CHIEF HICKEY

We don't have any evidence about any of her teachers.

DONALD HARDING

Well, what else was she into? Wasn't she in a play last year?

CHARLES PARKER

She had the lead in . . . whatever it was. *Oklahoma!*, I think. But if you think—

DONALD HARDING

Who directed it? Does anybody know?

ELIZABETH MAHLER

Ed Meskill. My son Lindon was in it. He's head of the sociology department and the drama club. He directs all the plays.

DONALD HARDING

What about him?

CHIEF HICKEY

We've interviewed him. He lives up the street. He's one of the neighbors we questioned to see if he heard anything that night.

DONALD HARDING

One of the neighbors, huh? What kind of an alibi does he have?

CHIEF HICKEY

Only that he was correcting papers in his study.

DONALD HARDING

No witnesses, huh? And it was his wife who called in about the stranger, that . . . Wilfred Greene. Maybe there're in it together. You think about that, Chief?

CHIEF HICKEY

We're thinking about everybody and anybody, and we're open to suggestion. But we have to have some evidence, or some reason to suspect anybody.

DONALD HARDING

No imagination! Hugh, Charlie, what do you think?

HUGH McCORMICK

You're talking about a play she was in a year ago.

CHARLES PARKER

She wasn't even in the drama club this year, she told me. She was into other things.

DONALD HARDING

What other things?

CHARLES PARKER

I don't know.

but an ignorant, well-meaning artifact who should have been put out to pasture fifteen years ago. Only they made him chief instead.

He would have been okay two generations ago, back when Crockford was a town of three thousand farmers and fishermen. There was no crime here back then. The only thing you'd need a cop for was to settle a dispute over who dented whose fender, or keep some lush from breaking up Willday's Saloon when Will wouldn't serve him another drink.

But Crockford's eighteen thousand now, and it's turned into an upper-middle-class town, not as rich as Madison, to the east of us, more like Guilford, to the west, a residence for New Haven's affluent. And where the affluent go, crime follows. And crime lives with us now. I don't just mean Sally Anders. I don't mean murder— but we've had a couple of those in recent years. I'm talking about theft, burglary, holdups. The Deli Mart on Route 1 got held up a year ago. And the Bottle Shop, Bill Daitch's place on River Street, right off the Green? That's been held up twice in the last five years! And, this year, two Route 1 gas-station holdups within a month of each other.

There are the burglaries! Especially in the homes out where I live on Clarkson Road. They're built in the woods, out of sight of each other. Well-to-do people like seclusion and being surrounded by trees and not being able to see or hear any neighbors. But that makes them pawns for robbers. And the cops know who some of those robbers are. But they don't arrest them. They claim they don't have evidence.

That's all right. I believe them. They don't have evidence. And that's what I'm talking about. We've got a police force that isn't suited to today's world. What we need, if we're going to stop the rise of crime around here, is a police force that will *get* evidence. Herb Hickey's a nice enough guy, but he's out of his depth in the Crockford of today. He doesn't like me because he knows I see through him. I know what he knows—that he ought to

HUGH McCORMICK

She sang in the choir in St. Bartholomew's Church. Are we now going to suspect Ethelbert Stallings because he's the choir director?

DONALD HARDING

Oh, hell, forget Stallings. I don't know why even his wife would go to bed with him.

CHIEF HICKEY

Well, now, we've had cases of some strange relationships. . . . I mean—I don't mean that we think there'd be anything between Mr. Stallings and Sally Anders. There's never been a hint of gossip about him.

DONALD HARDING

Nobody suspects Stallings, for Christ's sake. In fact, I don't think he's got enough reputation to need to try to hide an affair. If I were Stallings, I'd *brag* about it.

HUGH McCORMICK

Who's got a reputation, Don, you think *would* want to hide such a thing—enough to kill for?

DONALD HARDING

Open the phone book. There're hundreds of names.

CHIEF HICKEY
We can't go into this blind, Mr. Harding. Not unless you commissioners want to hire a couple of hundred more men.

HUGH McCORMICK
For a start, Don, what were *you* doing the evening of May seventh?

DONALD HARDING
How the hell should I know? You think I keep a diary?

HUGH McCORMICK
Now there's a suspicious character for you.

DONALD HARDING
Check with my wife. You want to pin me to the wall? She's the social secretary. It's all down in her calendar. Every move we make! You want to talk about alibis? She'll alibi me till the cows come home. If I go to the store, it's in her calendar. If I blow my nose, she's recorded it.

CHARLES PARKER
Maybe there're some people of reputation whose wives aren't as explicit as Don's. Maybe some can't account for what they did the evening of May the seventh.

CHIEF HICKEY

Like I say, we don't have the manpower to question the world. We have to limit ourselves to possibilities. We have to say, "Who might have had reason or opportunity to establish a relationship with the Anders girl, who might kill her to keep her from talking?" That's our problem.

DONALD HARDING

The minister of her church—Walter Wallace?

CHIEF HICKEY

Him? Why him?

DONALD HARDING

She was in the choir and other church things, youth groups and the like. You don't like Stallings for a suspect? How about Walter?

CHIEF HICKEY

Granting the affair, you think he'd *kill* her?

DONALD HARDING

Who knows what evil lurks in the hearts of men? And ministers aren't exempt.

CHIEF HICKEY

But Walter Wallace is married, has two children, and is one of the pillars of society.

DONALD HARDING

There's a reputation to uphold! *I'd* kill for that. What was Walter Wallace doing the night Sally was murdered?

CHIEF HICKEY

We don't know.

HUGH McCORMICK

I wonder if we *ought* to know.

CHARLES PARKER

Why? I mean, because she sang in the choir, was interested in the church?

HUGH McCORMICK

Maybe we should—Herb should—ask Dorothy Meskill to check it out. Dorothy's one of the church leaders.

DONALD HARDING

Hugh's got a point. Walter Wallace is a very attractive man. He leads the Fellowship group that's oriented toward the young people, and he takes a big interest in bringing in youth groups to build the church's future. I can see him as a father image, an idol image, for the church's young. He encourages the hell out of them, getting them involved. He's the kind of man someone like Sally could go for. He exudes the kind of charisma an innocent girl could fall in love with—be willing to die for.

HUGH McCORMICK
Now don't go overboard, Don. He's got six hundred parishioners he's responsible for. His reputation is untarnished. Are you suggesting he was seducing Sally on the side and killed her because she threatened to tell? I mean, we have to be realistic!

DONALD HARDING
I'm not suggesting anything. I'm only saying I'd like to know where Walter Wallace was the evening of May seventh!

HUGH McCORMICK
Probably home.

DONALD HARDING
Then let's get his wife to confirm it.

HUGH McCORMICK
Selma? You want Herb to ask Selma where Walter was that night?

DONALD HARDING

Why not? You want to know where *I* was? I didn't even *know* the Anders girl. But Walter Wallace did. And remember, Sally was hot for church. I mean, she was into the Fellowship group and she sang in the choir. Most girls her age you have to drag to church in handcuffs. She volunteered. That's strange on the face of it. I'd like to know why. Wouldn't you, Chief?

CHIEF HICKEY

Well, we have picked up that she was more interested in religion and the church than most girls her age. And we do recognize that she seemed to have a relationship with the minister that seemed closer than average. I repeat, that's not evidence. A lot of young people do get devoted to their church and get into church work, so her interest doesn't prove anything. However, it's something we do have to take into account. It's one of the things she was involved in, and we have to search out the reasons.

DONALD HARDING

Good hunting. I think maybe we're getting somewhere at last.

Thursday May 28

BERT RICHARDS

It's three weeks to the day now since Sally Anders got killed. Three weeks! And what do the police know about it? Nothing! Are they any closer to the killer? No. What have they done in these three weeks? Sowed a lot of dissent and alarm around town, caused more damned trouble than a herd of elephants.

I know what the cops think about me. They think I want to *get* them because they arrested my son. They think I've been trying to get appointed to the police commission to roll heads, get even with everybody involved in his arrest. That shows you what kind of a police department we've got. That shows you why I'm the pain in the rear I am.

Do I want to get on the police commission? You bet I do. And do I want to roll a few heads? You can bet on that, too. You get me on that police commission and the first thing I'd work my rear off to do would be to get rid of Herb Hickey! But it's nothing personal. I wouldn't fire him, I'd retire him. Why? Because he's nothing retire and let the town hire a police chief out of New Haven, or a retired captain of detectives out of New York; someone who'll put life into our police force, solve crimes for a change, and scare criminals into staying away from our town.

And let's get rid of that impossible wife of his who struts around like the Queen of England because her husband's the chief. Don't get in her way or she'll tell her husband and he'll fix you. Or so she thinks.

But they keep blocking my appointment to the commission. That's because they know I'd raise hell. They think it's a vendetta, but that's nonsense. I kick and fuss and shout because I care about this town. And the only way to get anything done is to yell and scream. It's the squeaky wheel that gets the grease. And I'm a squeaky wheel because, if all I did was sit back and write letters to the *Shoreline News,* nothing would happen. If you want to see changes made, you have to be willing to get in there and fight for those changes. Nobody ever wants to move all by himself. The inertia's too strong. You've got to light a firecracker under people to make them sit up and take notice. All right, I grant you the squeaky wheel is the unpopular wheel. People don't like it that I kick up a fuss. But I don't give a damn about being liked or disliked. Well, I've never really been liked, so maybe I don't know what I'm talking about. As for being disliked, I can tell you plenty. Ask my ex-wife. She can speak for days on how dislikable I am. So, how much worse off can I be? All that matters to me is setting things right. And if you're going to succeed in that, you've got to raise some hell.

But the police commissioners, they don't want any hell being raised. So they don't want my presence on their precious commission. And they don't want to get off the commission to make room for me either. Hugh McCormick, Charlie Parker and Don Harding? They love being on the Police Commission. All their lives they've been intimidated by policemen. Now the shoe's on the other foot. Now they intimidate the policemen.

And their wives love it too. They don't ever want their

husbands to get off. "Give me a ticket for illegal parking? I beg your pardon. Do you know who I am?" And the patrolman says, "Sorry, ma'am, my mistake."

But that's no reason for being a commissioner, or a commissioner's wife. I've studied police work. I've read up on the latest techniques. So, when I do get on the commission—and that's going to happen (I've paid my dues to the party)—I'll know what the job is all about. Hugh and Charlie and Don serve on the commission, but they don't know their business. They have to learn it from Herb Hickey. That's the trouble with most of the commissions in town. The Board of Education interviews and hires a superintendent of schools and then rubber-stamps every recommendation he makes. The same with the police commission. They say, "What do you recommend, Herb?" and think what he tells them is straight from God. Because they don't know any better.

And what have we got?

The most hideous murder that's ever happened in this town took place three weeks ago and nobody has any idea who the killer is. All anybody does is point a finger and say, "How about him?" And what's that got us?

Reggie Sawyer Senior, principal of Dudley Bishop Elementary School, the best damned principal this town has ever seen, has quit! And he doesn't even know where he's going next! But he quit—resigned at a Board of Education meeting two nights ago.

And listen to what we've lost!

What he could do to bring out the best in teachers, to make the children in his charge love to come to school and learn, you wouldn't believe! He was one of the things that made Crockford great. People with young children paid whatever it took to move to Crockford just so their kids could have the benefit of our educational system, and they picked their houses so their kids could go to his school!

And now he's leaving. He's turning his back on us. And I don't blame him.

The idea that anyone—anyone—could suspect his son

of having anything to do with Sally's death is beyond the realm of belief.

Young Reggie? A top athlete, a top scholar, president of his class, three Ivy League scholarships awaiting him? Along with God knows how many athletic scholarships to those football factories that concentrate on winning teams and the hell with burdening their prize players with such things as classwork.

The world was his oyster. He was the God damned pride of Crockford, to the degree that Crockford has any right to be proud. He's gone, and his father's gone, and Crockford will never be the same again.

So, the finger pointed and we lost two of our best.

And now what's been happening? Where are the fingers pointing now? People are saying, "What about Walter Wallace, the pastor of St. Bartholomew's Church?" "And what about Sally's teachers?" Ever since it's come out that Sally carried condoms around, everybody's looking for a "lover." And it's got to be an "older man." Now that they've dispensed with Reggie Sawyer, they're turning their attention to every adult in town she's done more than say hello to.

Walter Wallace? What have they got on him? Nothing, except that he doesn't have an alibi for the night she was murdered. I'm on the vestry at St. Bartholomew's Church and I've been witness. He thinks he was making house calls, but it isn't listed on his appointment book. Lacking that, he doesn't remember. All we know is his wife doesn't know either, for she was hosting a Ladies' Aid Society supper in the parish house which he was supposed to appear at later to say a few words. But he didn't show up.

So the fingers start pointing at him. Why? Because Sally was interested in church activities; because he and she were seen discussing things together; and he has a lousy alibi for the night she was killed.

What the hell are we talking about here? We've got innuendo, elaboration, jumping to conclusions. It's all speculation as to what might have happened.

Does anybody stop to think what kind of a man Walter

Wallace is? He's married. He has two children. He's dedicated to his religion. I know him better than most, being on the vestry, and I have to say, if he could rape and murder Sally Anders, I belong back in kindergarten learning all over again what's what in this world. He's not a lecher. He is, in fact, a fearful man. I don't think he can stand without a prop. I have the feeling he clings to religion as the source of his be-all and end-all. I don't really know where he'd be without it.

And since Sally's death, and particularly now, when he can't produce hard and sure evidence as to where he was that evening, he wears a haunted look. He's aware of the whispers that are going around, and he's totally incapable, out of his own *being*, to rise up and blow them away. He's at sea, not because he welcomed Sally's interest in church activities, but because he can't produce an ironclad alibi.

So, Godammit, let's demand that everybody in town produce an ironclad alibi for May the seventh, and anybody who can't becomes a suspect. There you are, Herb Hickey. There's your suspect list!

What did I do on the evening of May seventh?

How the hell should I know?

Make what you want of that, Hickey!

Tuesday June 9

EMILY DAITCH

I can't believe it. I simply can't believe it. And that remark's coming from *me*! Don't I know everything that goes on in this town? Are there any secrets I don't know about? I would've sworn there weren't.

But still waters run deep. Wow, do they run deep! I never would have suspected! And that says something, because I pride myself. I'm a damned good reporter. And, as I always say, the reason I know everybody's secret is because everybody knows and trusts me. Everybody knows I won't tell.

Well, nobody else suspected it either. Not that that means anything. That doesn't justify my not even having an inkling! How could anybody be so clever? I hate to admit it, but I was completely taken in. So was everybody else—but I have pride. I can smell a rat by instinct. It comes from being a reporter for so long, from knowing so many people, from knowing so many things about so many people. Maybe the fault was mine. Maybe I got careless. Maybe I thought I knew so much

200

about so many people that I knew everything about everybody.

You develop a second sense in my business. You get so you can tell if someone isn't being forthcoming, if someone's trying to keep something from you. I've covered so many stories in my years with the *Shoreline News*, interviewed so many people, seen them in all their off moments, half dressed; grieving at a bedside; wanting to kill an errant husband; wishing their children were dead and they were free to start again; wanting to kill themselves! I have to tell you, there are three women in this town I personally talked out of killing themselves. I'm not going to tell you their stories because, like I say, I keep secrets. But there are three women walking the streets of this town today who wouldn't be here if I hadn't listened to them, consoled them, tried my damnedest— and I don't know anything about psychology except what I've learned from living, for what *that's* worth—to talk them out of it.

On two occasions, it was over coffee in the kitchen. One woman was in her bathrobe, and she couldn't stop fingering the chef's knife from her kitchen drawer. She'd drawn its blade razor keen on the electric sharpener and she kept testing it—very carefully—drawing her finger along its sides so only the tip of her finger grazed the edge—just enough to know the slightest pressure would draw blood. She kept doing this while she talked, and my heart was in my mouth. I mean literally! When someone's in that much trouble, who knows what they'll do? I mean, say a wrong word and she might turn the knife on me. And it had the sharpest point! I didn't even see her while we talked. All I could see was the point of the knife, aiming my way across the table.

A reporter doesn't just report. Sometimes you find yourself involved in your stories. I mean *involved*.

But I'm not mentioning names. None of them did it— killed herself. And their husbands don't know they even thought about it. At least, they didn't hear anything about it from me. Nobody heard anything about it from me, including Doctor Allen. I'm not trying to shape the world— make things come out right—. I'm only trying to report what happens—after it happens. And these times it didn't happen.

This is only to say I know my way around this town. I know what goes on. Or I thought I did.

But this thing threw me. Really *threw* me. And what I'm telling you now isn't betraying any confidence, because I didn't find it out and I didn't report it. Detective Harris found it out and it's all over town. Don't ask me how the word got out. Martha Hickey told me that Jack Harris and Chief Hickey and the commissioners and everybody else who got told what Jack found swear they never breathed a word.

But that's this town. Nobody can keep a secret—except me. Let the police discover something and everybody's going to know what it is. That's the police department for you. Somebody whispers—somebody tells his wife, or a dearest friend—and the word is out. I'm not suggesting who blabbed, but I have an idea. One of the police commissioners whispered it to his wife. I think I know who the wife was, but I can't say for sure and I'm not going to mention any names or cast any suspicions.

Anyway, since it's no secret anymore, I can tell you what happened. Detective Jack Harris was the one who found it out. Nothing against him. He's a fine detective. I think he's the best man on the force—the most dedicated.

So there's this horrible murder mystery in town. Who could have raped and killed Sally Anders? Nobody's been able to sleep for wondering. And the fingers have been pointing and people have been asking each other: "Could it have been so-and-so?" or "Where was so-and-so the night of May seventh?"

And some of the fingers were pointing to Walter Wallace, the priest at St. Bartholomew's Church. Not for any other reason than because Sally Anders had become quite involved in church activities over the last couple of years, which isn't usual for teenage girls, except, maybe, as a

way to meet boys with the same interest. I mean, if you're
a well-brought-up girl in a goldfish-bowl kind of town like
Crockford, and you want to meet boys, getting involved in
church activities is one of the ways to do it—one of the
better ways. The boys you meet share the same religion,
which is always a good thing, and they have an interest in
God and moral behavior—or you hope they do, though I
can tell you it's a two-way street and a lot of them get
involved for the same reason a girl does—to meet people
of the opposite sex. In any case, it's one of the better ways
of playing the mating game, which is what all teenagers
are doing, no matter what else they may tell you. Even if
they don't know it themselves.

Well, it was recognized that Walter Wallace was good-
looking and charismatic, and that she and he were friendly—
had talks together. There was no evidence that the
relationship was any more than pastor and flock, and
probably nothing would've come of it, except that Walter
Wallace didn't have an alibi for what he did the evening of
May seventh. Usually his calendar would list his schedule,
and if he were home, his wife could confirm it. But this
particular date was a blank. He couldn't remember the
day, could only believe he made calls, but he didn't know
on whom or why. He wasn't home. He and his wife
agreed to that. That was all he could say.

Now, without any evidence against him, or any reason to suspect him, nobody would pay attention to his
lapse of memory. Hell, not one person in ten could
remember what they'd done two days ago, let alone two
weeks.

But it bugged Jack Harris. I asked him about it
after and he couldn't tell me a good reason why he
did what he did, except that Sally Anders was dead
and there weren't any suspects at all. As Jack put it,
"Everybody's above suspicion, but somebody did it. Somebody's guilty, and maybe it's like the old-fashioned
mystery stories where the least-suspected person is the
villain."

Jack Harris was the only one bothered by Walter Wallace's lack of an alibi. "The guy's schedule is ironclad," he told me. "Every appointment is listed, every call he makes is recorded afterward." So Jack Harris went over Walter's appointment book, with Walter's permission and in Walter's presence, and he didn't say anything to Walter about it, but he noted the appointment book wasn't airtight all the way through. May seventh wasn't the *only* evening that couldn't be accounted for by an appointment, a meeting, a church call, or an evening at home with his family.

As I say, Jack only looked over the book and nodded and let Walter believe he was satisfied. But he didn't like those unexplained evenings. What was Walter doing during those unrecorded hours? They didn't form any pattern— like Wednesday night bowling, or a change in the porno flicks in East Haven—but they were there, lying in the past, and Jack Harris decided there'd be more of them in the future.

So Jack started staking out Walter's house. This wasn't orders from the chief. This was strictly on his own, his own time, without any chits for expenses, without telling anybody what he was doing, except his wife. She didn't like it and he wouldn't have told her, except he had to have some reason for going out nights when he was off-duty.

And last Wednesday night, the night of June third, after he'd been following Walter on routine stuff since May twenty-ninth, he tailed Walter to Laird Armstrong's house, and I guess you know what *that* means. Laird lives alone with his invalid aunt in that big barn of a homestead on Hartford Street. Laird never married; says it's because he spent his twenties caring for his bedridden mother and his thirties looking after his dying father. Nobody questions that. We all nod and let it go at that. Because Laird is a helluva nice guy, active in the Art League, president of the Chamber Music Society, is one of the leading underwriters of our Crockford Concert series, plays the organ in the Congregational Church, and, above all, he's discreet. He's gay but he does his utmost not to let it show. Around town, you wouldn't ever know it, except for the little signs that somebody who's that way can't completely hide. What he does and whom he entertains behind the closed doors of that big house nobody's ever wanted to know. That's his own private business and we didn't give a damn.

Except that Jack Harris tailed Walter Wallace to the Armstrong mansion and waited two hours for him to come out. And this was no church call. Laird isn't Episcopalian.

Wednesday June 10

WALTER WALLACE

I don't know how it happened, why anybody would want to follow me, see where I'm going, what I'm doing. It's parish calls, church meetings, and, when I can manage it, a quiet evening at home with my wife and children—a little television maybe. And why would anybody want to broadcast it around town? I suppose I've got enemies. I don't know of any, but whatever ones I've got aren't going to tell me. They'll just quietly help the ax to fall. But don't they know what they're doing to other people? Don't they know the damage they do to the innocents? And the damage . . . the damage . . .

Jack Harris claims it wasn't he who told. He's the one who found me out. Jack Harris, the spy, the betrayer. My Judas Iscariot. "Only doing his duty," he says. I pray for his soul. If he was really doing his duty, he could've kept his mouth shut. He only wanted to know what I was doing the night of May seventh, when poor Sally Anders was so brutally murdered. But why me? He says it's because I didn't have an alibi and I was friendly with Sally and there

was talk. What talk? I never heard any talk! And friendly
with Sally? Of course I was friendly with Sally. And with
Peggy and Jack Welch and Carl Masters and Julie Broad-
street and all the other young people who come to our
church and participate in our youth programs. That's what
I try to do in this church—get the young people involved.
I've seen too many ministers take on a new congregation
and devote themselves to the older members, the ones
who have commitment, who have money, who're devoted
to the church, who're the backbone of the laity, who raise
the funds and contribute the funds to make the church
run. But they get older and older, and what's going to
happen when they die?

"Look to the youth" is my credo. Develop attractive
programs for the young. Make church not just a religious
experience, but a fun experience. Worshiping God doesn't
have to be painful. It doesn't pleasure God to have us
abrade our knees on hard floors or get arthritis sitting in
uncomfortable pews. Torturing ourselves isn't how He
wants us to serve Him. He wants us to *work* for Him, not
suffer for Him.

But don't think I haven't had trouble propounding that
philosophy. The laity is full of old fogies who don't want
children to enjoy religion, who don't want them to feel
that God is *fun* to get to know. They claim I'm trying to
sugarcoat the Faith to make it palatable, that the worship
of God should be its own reward, that wanting to love and
follow Jesus is how we lift ourselves, and that we've got to
do the lifting *by* ourselves or it doesn't have any meaning.
They think youth groups and picnics and Bible discussion
groups are crutches. They claim that gets the kids into
it for the social end, and that's not what religion's all
about.

But I say you can't get young people to love Jesus by
telling them they *ought* to, or by saying they won't be
saved if they don't. I want them to find out for themselves
that Jesus is someone to love. I want them to love Jesus as
I love Jesus, and that's a feeling that has to come from
within! It's the most wonderful feeling in the world, and

it's not something everybody can experience, not even all
those who try. It's a special kind of joy, and I want to
share it with as many people as I can—and especially with
the young. Because they're the easiest to reach. They
haven't closed off all the doors or thrown up insurmount-
able blockades.

And they're the hope of the future. Get the young
people to church and you'll have a *strong* church!

But, as I say, there're many in the church who don't
agree. And there are those, I see now, who want me out.
I wouldn't have believed the feeling was that intense.
And now they have their chance. All because Judas
Iscariot, in the guise of Jack Harris, was following me last
Wednesday.

Jack didn't have to ask Laird Armstrong on Thursday
to confirm I'd been at his house the night of May
seventh. The fact I went to Laird's house *any* night
should have been evidence enough that I hadn't attacked
Sally!

But Jack said he had to be thorough. Not that it would
have mattered if he hadn't gone back to see Laird, I
suppose, except that it was so embarrassing to Laird.
Laird's never had to admit to anything before. Everybody
knew, but everybody pretended.

And Jack swears to me he couldn't keep quiet about it.
He *tried*, he said. He assured Hickey I was clear. But
Hickey wouldn't take his word for it without knowing
why. Hickey can't stand secrecy. He's got to be in the
know. Hickey told Jack that, because the commissioners
were suspecting me, he couldn't tell them to forget it
without telling them why. Those police commissioners are
even worse than Hickey that way. I suppose that's why
they become commissioners—so they can know all the
dirt and slime and ugliness that goes on in this supposedly
saintly town!

So Hickey had to know, and the commissioners had to
know. And Jack Harris had to tell them. That's how he
alibis himself.

Never mind that Hickey and the commissioners swore

they'd never tell. You know what promising secrecy means. It wasn't two days before the story was all over town.

When I was a kid, growing up, I didn't know I was different. I thought I was an ordinary little boy, just like all the other little boys. I suppose one of the troubles was I didn't have friends with whom to compare myself.

I wasn't rugged and athletic like most of the others. I didn't like to push and shove. I couldn't play in their games. I tried a few times—I really *wanted* to be like them. But I was *so* inept. It was embarrassing. I felt shamed.

So I dropped out. But I didn't think being unathletic made me different. A lot of other boys weren't athletic either.

But how I envied the ones who were. I was drawn to them. I wished I could be like them. But, as far as I knew, so did all the other boys like me who couldn't make the team.

Thank the Good Lord I didn't know what my problem was back then. I wouldn've been terrified at what I was feeling. What I was feeling was, I loved the look of men, of their strong, rock-hard bodies. Girls were so soft. I didn't like their softness. When I lay in bed at night, my thoughts were about boys, about the way they behaved and acted. They were more interesting to me than girls. I was drawn to them, not to girls.

But I thought that was normal. I saw it at school— the boys ganged together, played handball against the side of the school gym during lunch period, and the girls gathered on the gym fire-escape alongside and giggled and gabbed and ignored the boys, and the boys ignored the girls and played their game. That's what I thought. I didn't know back then *why* the girls gathered on the fire escape, *why* the boys pretended the girls weren't there and the girls pretended the boys weren't there.

If I'd really been normal, I would've known it was all

pretense. The boys knew what every girl was doing, especially the ones they liked, and the girls knew what every
boy was doing, especially the ones *they* liked.

And at the few parties I got to go to, I noticed how all
the boys were on one side of the room, the girls on the
other, and half the party would be over before they began
to mingle.

And because I didn't have any close friends—boys I
could talk to—I learned how to behave from what I saw.
There was nobody to tell me different. What I saw was
that boys liked girls and dated girls and proposed to girls
and married girls and had children. That was the way it
was done.

And that's the way I did it. I dated girls. I held their
hands and tried to kiss them. In college, hearing in bull
sessions about the further sexual pleasures to be enjoyed,
I explored further and, back then, the climate was permis-
sive. The girls expected, even encouraged it. I lost my
virginity at nineteen—rather late by peer-group standards—
but I was used to running behind. The one thing I found
troubling was that, even when I'd done it, it wasn't all
that great. The other boys rhapsodized about the experience. They couldn't talk about anything but girls and sex.
And I'd done it, but I hadn't had the same thrill. I found
myself more excited watching and listening to the other
boys talk than to what we'd all done. I wondered for a
while if it wasn't showmanship, a pleasure in the achieve-
ment rather than in the act itself. Bedding down a girl was
all right, but it wasn't all that exciting. Surely, they were
making it up.

I didn't encounter the word *homosexual* until my sophomore year. It was bandied about with laughter and ridi-
cule one evening. I didn't know what it meant, and I
didn't ask. In bull sessions I only listened and tried to
learn what my proper responses ought to be.

But I remembered the word and looked it up, to know
what the other boys were talking about.

And then came the awful feeling! Was I an errant one
in this group? Could it possibly be that the reason I didn't

lust after women, that I didn't get the pleasure from them that all the other boys claimed to, that I was attracted to men's hard-muscled bodies and didn't drool over pictures of soft, naked females, that I had a yearning to be with males, without knowing quite why, was because I really was different from all the others? Could it possibly be that I was a *homosexual*?

I fought it. I didn't want to be different. I wanted to be like everybody else.

I suppose anybody, reading this, will wonder why I chose the ministry, query whether this horrible feeling I had made me turn to the church for help. I don't know. Right now, under this albatross, I cannot judge what I think.

My dear wife, Selma, married me while I was in the seminary studying for the ministry. We've been married eighteen years and our children are Peter, twelve, and Mary, eight. We waited six years to have children because of the uncertainty of the future.

It's been a happy marriage—by her standards. (She confessed that to me last night.) It was a happy one, as best I could make it, by mine.

We had to have a talk, of course. I had to admit my lie.

You have to understand how it was. Maybe it's my fault, but I so wanted to *belong*. I'd've given anything to be like everybody else. All I wanted to do was finish my preparation for the priesthood, marry a proper girl, settle down, raise children, preach the Faith and, as an example as well as a preacher, try to brighten the corner where I lived. Crockford was the parish to which I was assigned, and I wanted to help make Crockford the finest place in the world for anyone to want to live. Ambitious? Yes. I've been ambitious! I've wanted to leave a mark on things. I've wanted to make the world better for my having passed through it.

And all the while, there's been that evil in me, that estrangement. I don't know how to describe it, except as the mark of the Devil. I fought it. I married, did all the

right things, was true to my wife, raised children—and all
the while there was this dissatisfaction within me.

I fought that too. Who says the world is supposed to
satisfy? God promised us salvation, but He didn't promise
us a rose garden.

I'm a sinner. I'm not strong enough. I met Laird Armstrong. Everybody in town meets Laird Armstrong. He's a
part of the town. And something happened. I don't know
what. But Laird is the kindest, gentlest, most Godlike
person I've ever known. We related, he and I. In ways I
couldn't ever relate to Selma. She was a woman and Laird
was a man, and that was the ultimate difference. I found in
Laird all that had been missing in my relationship with
women. The thrill, the ecstasy that my classmates in
college talked about experiencing with women, and which
I could not understand, I found in Laird. Suddenly, with
him, a whole new wondrous world opened up. It wasn't
just a meeting of bodies, it was a meeting of minds as
well. I discovered, with Laird, such happiness as I could
not have imagined before. It was a happiness so great as
to make any risk worth the taking.

I had a loving wife and two children dearer to me than
life itself. I had a mission, a job to do. What more could
any man ask?

Yet I was willing to risk it all for stolen evenings with
another man! Can anyone understand that? I cannot. Except to believe that Evil has been born in me and lies
heavier on my soul than my ability to cast it out.

I tried the Devil's trick—solacing myself in my evil
while pretending to be good. And, as is God's will, the
evil will be found out. All evil thoughts will be discovered, all evil actions disclosed.

My wife rants against me. In another cause, she would
have stood by my side, even at the Gates of Hell. "What
am I to do?" she cries. "Against another woman, I would
bear arms. I could *fight* another woman. I would stand a
chance against another woman! But what can I do against
another man? I am helpless and unarmed against another
man!"

And my children? Peter and Mary, named for the holy ones I worship? They avoid me. They look the other way. I don't think they know what all this means, but they know things I did not know at their age, and maybe the horror is upon them as well. Whatever the case, they hide—perhaps from the reality they don't want to have to face? In any case, from me.

I owe an apology to Jack Harris. He is *not* Judas Iscariot, betraying Christ, he is the Angel of God, exposing evil in the world.

The Bishop wants to see me. My whole world has fallen.

What purpose, oh God, was I to serve, that You should make me this way?

Thursday June 11

They found him in the steeple. He was hanging from the main beam beside the plank stairs to the bells.

They didn't know where he'd gone.

Let us hear from Selma Wallace, Walter's wife.

SELMA WALLACE

Well, I don't know. I don't know anything anymore. I don't *feel* anything anymore. Walter and I were married eighteen years. You think you get to know a man in eighteen years. We married when he was halfway through theological seminary. We were going together before he went in. We were going together back in high school. I met him at a sorority dance. He came with Jocelyn Palmer and I was with Barry Jackson. It was back when drugs and hippies and love beads were the thing. Down with the establishment! That sort of thing.

I was never into the rebellion of the sixties. I had a strict upbringing and an inborn respect for authority. When I was little, if a policeman so much as looked my way, I had the feeling he was reading my soul and knew all my sins, and I worried what I might have done that he would arrest me for.

And teachers! They were kings and queens, and I tried to do everything they said, tried my best to earn their appreciation. I heard the term "brownnosing," and I sensed some students applied it to me. I didn't know exactly what it meant, except that it was derogatory. But I wasn't being nice to teachers, and obedient and unquestioning, because I wanted good marks. I truly believed they were the fonts from which wisdom came. They were grown-ups, and grown-ups, unlike children, never made mistakes. And if I tried to do what they told me to do, I'd grow up and not make any mistakes either. And I made so many mistakes when I was little. I couldn't sew straight. I missed corners when I dusted, no matter how hard I tried. My grandmother raised me, and she was a grown-up. *She* never made mistakes. She sewed a straight line, and she knew every corner that needed dusting.

Barry Jackson was different. But, so far as I knew, all boys were. He was careless and slipshod. He never shined his shoes, never combed his hair—well, almost never. He'd run a hand through it and that was that. But the way it came out was kind of appealing. He was the cutest boy in the class. All of us girls were crazy about him.

And I invited him to this sorority dance we were throwing. I mean, it wasn't out of a clear blue sky. We knew each other. We'd dated before. Not that he didn't date a lot of different girls, but he seemed very glad that I invited him to the dance. Not that he wouldn't have been invited by half a dozen other girls if I hadn't been first.

But Barry had this wild streak. He drank and smoked pot and was into LSD. At least that's what they said. And he talked back to teachers and he'd already been suspended from school twice when I knew him. There was also talk about him getting a girl in trouble, but I don't know if that was true. He never tried to do anything with me or any of the other girls I knew.

The real trouble with Barry, though, was that you never knew where you stood. You could invite him to a dance, as girls always did, and he'd come for you and take you home, and he'd present you with a corsage, which you weren't expecting since you'd done the inviting and the dance was supposed to be on you. But once you got there, he hardly seemed to know you anymore. He had so many friends, boys and girls, that he was always mingling—leaving you to go see this person or that person. He'd always come back, but you had the feeling the party was the attraction, not you. And he'd take you home and give you a chaste good-night kiss and thank you and tell you how wonderful it was, and all the while you wished he'd kiss you as if you were special and tell you it was *you* who made the evening so wonderful. But he never did. Not to me, and not to any of the other girls I talked to.

Anyway, it was at this dance that I met Walter. Jocelyn told me she *had* to take him, that it had to be someone her parents approved of. She was really after Barry, but I'd got him first, and they wouldn't have let her invite him anyway. But she got me to swap dances and somehow Walter and I got left together for a while.

It wasn't for all that long, but we talked a little and I found out he was shy and afraid, and it touched me because that's the way I was too.

We ended up on the veranda, talking. He told me he was going to go to college, and he didn't know what he wanted to do after that. That made an impression on me because I wanted to go to college too, and *do* something with my life. Barry would never go to college. He bragged about quitting school. He could get a job pumping gas at the Atlas filling station any time he wanted, he claimed, and he'd end up owning the station and then a string of stations. He was going to be a gas-station tycoon and make millions.

I don't know how to explain it, except I sensed that, while Barry might thrill me, he was a dead end. We didn't share anything in common. It was only physical attraction and, young as I was back then, I somehow sensed that

that wasn't enough—enough for now, maybe, but not enough for a lifetime.

But kind, shy Walter, who had dreams and ambitions, who felt the kind of fears and hopes I felt, this was a man I was drawn to. And he had charm. It didn't show much then, when he was so shy and vulnerable. But as he grew and developed and gained confidence in himself—never enough confidence, and perhaps now I understand why—he was a real charmer. But mostly for the ladies. Now, when I think back about it, his charm was mostly for the ladies. Men accepted him. I never heard a word against him. But he didn't attract the men. He dealt with them, made friends of them—the men are, after all, the bulwark of the Church. It's the men's money, not the Women's Aid Society, that makes the church function.

We dated, got to know each other, and I was there when he got The Call, when he decided his future lay in the ministry. It wouldn't have been my choice. I didn't want to be a minister's wife. Your life's not your own. The minister's wife lives in and with the church, and I was never that much of a churchgoer. I went because my parents took me, and I obeyed their dictates and tried to like what they made me do. But religion was hard for me to swallow. There're people who revel in religion. There're people, like Walter, who live it. And I couldn't care less. I feel closer to God watching squirrels climb trees, watching birds fly, hearing the peepers in the spring, seeing a gorgeous sunset. I'll drive the car to the edges of town to see a sunset. There's all the God I can want wherever I turn. And, in bed at night, I talk to Him direct. Never mind all this Jesus and Mary business. I talk to Him direct. I don't believe God is so highfaluting you can only approach Him through emissaries.

But I loved this shy, intellectual, dedicated man. He wanted so much to do so much. And he could do more than I. I don't mean that to sound antifeminist, I really mean it. He had strengths I knew I didn't have. All you have to do is hear the news that's going around town, how he fought against the Devil in his own life, and maybe

would have succeeded if he'd been given a little more
time. Maybe if he'd had a more understanding wife, more
understanding friends . . .

Now he's gone. I take the blame. I wasn't there when
he needed me. I was one of those who berated him. I was
so shocked and so hurt—so defensive, so helpless. I felt
justified. And I was so *wrong*!

Walter was deserted. He felt even his God had deserted him. If only one person—just one human being—
had stood by his side, had given him courage, had let him
know that he wasn't entirely alone, all of this horror might
have been avoided.

And *I* was that one person. I was the one who failed
him.

I'd always thought myself an ideal wife. I loved my
husband, I sacrificed my own goals and ambitions to help
him achieve his. How more noble can you get? I went
with him through college, when I thought he'd become a
doctor or a lawyer or an engineer. But those weren't his
leanings. He didn't know what his leanings were, nor did
I, but I was committed to his unknown ambitions. "Whither
thou goest, I shall go." To me, what more noble senti-
ment could a woman utter?

And when he chose the Church—the Episcopal Church—
which was a different form of Protestantism than I knew—
more Catholic than Protestant to my belief—I accepted
his choice and adjusted my life to that kind of future.

I have the uneasy feeling that I've failed in that. I mean
that, while I've been a dutiful wife—at least I'd fancied
myself a dutiful wife, until now, when I begin to wonder if
I've been any kind of a wife at all—but while I was what I
thought was a proper wife for an Episcopalian priest, I've
sensed that the congregation, the people who need and
support my husband, haven't taken to me. I've tried. God
knows how I've tried. You have to do so much, be so
much, as the wife of an Episcopal priest. It's like being
the First Lady. You weren't elected to the post. It was
forced upon you. And all eyes are upon *you*, more you than

your husband, the man who's supposed to be the focal point. All eyes—all women's eyes—are upon you. And what is expected of *you*?

I tried to prepare myself while Walter was going to the seminary. He was learning how to become a priest, and I was trying to learn how to become a priest's wife. And it was hard. It was by rote, not instinct. I'd been outgrowing my instincts. I'd been losing my respect for authority as I grew up. Parents, teachers, policemen, bosses weren't sacrosanct after all. Like Alice in Wonderland, I'd come to realize, "You're nothing but a pack of cards." And the same, I realized, went for the clergy. Vestments and rituals didn't proclaim truth.

It might have been easier to accept the tenets of the Episcopal Church if I'd been brought up in that church. But I hadn't been. The emphases and stresses were different. I'd been brought up believing what Jesus *said* was what was important, not who He was. Now I had to believe what He *was* was what was important, not what He said. It makes you wonder what you ought to believe, or if you ought to believe anything at all. I don't know, right now, if I even believe in God. A *Just* God, a *Righteous* God wouldn't allow the things that happen to happen.

So my faith wasn't strong. Try as I would, I couldn't become a devout Episcopalian. I pretended to be, for Walter's sake. I did all the proper things, proclaimed the proper doctrines, parroted the latest orthodoxy, or I thought I did. But maybe it showed. Maybe some quirk in voice or manner told the devout that I wasn't really one of them. Walter charmed them, but I did not. He was dedicated, and they knew they were in the presence of someone holier than themselves.

Until the terrible day a week ago when the world found out that Walter, too, had feet of clay. And, worse than that, that his sin was the most heinous in the lore of the church. Murder, adultery, betrayal can all be forgiven if one truly repents. But homosexuality is beyond the pale.

But who am I to talk? I was as shocked and bitter and outraged by the discovery as the most ardent and unforgiving worshiper. I felt I had lived in sin for eighteen years. I felt unclean. I cringed at the thought that this man had put his hands on me, that I had slept with him and borne his children. I wasn't thinking of him, I was thinking of me, and the disgrace. How could I face the world again? What could I say to my children?

I banished him from the bedroom. What else? He slept in his study those last days. After the first bitter recriminations—the words I said to him I'll curse till I die—we hardly spoke. I don't blame him for his silence. I wish I'd been silent. I wish I could take back those awful words, wipe away his ashen, stricken look. I ranted and railed about my suffering without noticing how much greater was his own. It was etched on his face and I never saw it.

And this morning, I didn't see him. Usually he'd be in and out of the house—make himself a cup of coffee, fix a sandwich for his lunch, picking times when I wasn't around. He didn't want his presence to exacerbate my wounds. But I'd hear him moving about. Or I'd see the signs of his presence—a coffee cup, carefully washed, standing in the dish drain, or a plate or knife, equally clean; a scattering of bread crumbs on the counter. Normally I cleaned up after him, for he was careless. But now he was trying not to inconvenience me, trying to make himself invisible. Except, the poor dear man, he didn't put things back on the shelves, and he forgot the bread crumbs. So I knew he was around.

Except today.

Today there wasn't a sign of him.

I thought at first I must have missed him, that he took his coffee in the parish house. But he didn't come home for lunch, and suddenly the house had this terrifying emptiness about it. I started looking for him. He wasn't in his study, of course, but I couldn't tell from the look of it if he'd slept there last night.

I hurried over to the parish house and asked Esther Stallings where Mr. Wallace was, and she hadn't seen him all day. Neither had Priscilla Webber, the church secretary, in the office downstairs. He hadn't taken the car out, so he had to be around. I asked them to help me find him, and we looked all over—the church, the parish house. I even tried the coffee shop across the Green, where he'd sometimes go, except I knew that's the last place he'd show his face after the word got out about him and Laird Armstrong.

He wasn't anywhere, and I had this sense of doom. It was if a light had gone out. I knew he was dead, just as surely as I breathed. But I didn't know where.

I called the police, to say I hadn't seen him and was worried. I thought they'd pooh-pooh me, but Sergeant McCrory was very serious and said they'd make inquiries. And he didn't tell me he was sure Walter would turn up all right. I think he had the same feeling I did.

It was Lucy Stedman who found him. She's one of the dedicated choir members. Large Lucy. She was a member of the choir before Walter came to St. Bartholomew's, and she's never missed a Sunday, or a rehearsal, not even when her husband died. I don't know why she went into the room off the choir dressing room where the steps go up to the steeple, and she doesn't know now either what made her do it. It's dim there, for the only natural light comes down the shaft from the bell windows at the top. She was the first to show up for choir practice, and for some reason she opened that door.

What she saw looked like a pair of legs hanging by the steps. She went in farther and saw that the legs were Walter's, that his body was dangling from a beam. With that, she let out a scream and fainted dead away.

I heard the scream. I was in the house, but I heard it. Everybody up and down the Green must have heard it. When Large Lucy screams, she screams.

I didn't know who screamed, and I didn't know where, but I knew what the scream meant. Walter had been found.

Monday June 15

The shock of Walter Wallace's suicide made everybody forget for a bit the murder of Sally Anders. For the record, Walter's death occurred five weeks to the day after Sally's. Both were on a Thursday and, in both cases, the funerals were on the Sunday following.

Sermons in the area churches that morning of June fourteenth dealt with the loss to the town of someone like Walter Wallace, with no mention made about his fall from grace. In today's world, even in a town like Crockford, Walter's relationship with Laird Armstrong, except in the eyes of the church, didn't seem all that sinful.

Not that Sally's murder had been forgotten. Walter's suicide was an aberration. Her death was a demon. Not only did the horror and nature of it freeze the soul, the mystery of it sensitized the mind. Who did it? If no one knew, no one could be sure it wouldn't happen again. The knowledge that "a killer walks among us" gripped the town with suspicion and fear.

Nor had anything been done in the ensuing five weeks to dispel either. The opportunity was unknown, the motive was unknown, the murderer was unknown. The most frightful crime in Crockford history remained as much a mystery as ever.

The police were supposed to be investigating. They *had* investigated. But now, though they wouldn't admit it publicly, the case was on hold. They had no clues. And they were intimidated! Where they'd cast suspicious eyes, havoc had followed; and their victims had been innocent. Public outrage was almost as great at what they'd done as at what they hadn't done. From the police standpoint, it was almost better to leave the case alone than to bungle it so badly.

The belabored police commissioners—Hugh McCormick, Don Harding and Charlie Parker—no longer so happy in their positions of prestige, steadfastly denied that police department investigations were to blame for the unfortunate aftermaths. They protested that Chief Hickey and his men were only doing their job. The commissioners were harder put, however, trying to explain the fact that the department's desperate fingers had condemned only innocent citizens and might condemn more!

The commissioners and the police backed off. They were afraid to probe into the background of any more respected citizens without solid, concrete evidence to justify it. And solid, concrete evidence was what they lacked.

Monday, the fifteenth of June, was graduation day for Crockford High. The ceremonies were held on the Green at six in the evening, in bright sunshine. Two hundred and sixty-four seniors were awarded their diplomas by Hugh Gibson, chairman of the Board of Education, in front of the teachers, the staff, and eleven hundred parents, relatives, friends and citizens.

You all know what graduations are like: everybody happy and proud, caps and gowns everywhere, the boys' gowns green, the girls' white. And the mood is upbeat, although there are tears in a lot of eyes and an occasional catch in the voice. And when it's over, there's the picture-taking, the hundreds of cameras, the thousands of snapshots. And the embracing; parents and graduates, graduates and graduates. "We'll be friends forever." "Write as soon as you arrive at college." "Keep in touch."

It's a happy time, and this graduation was a happy time, but you could sense it, all the same. It wasn't like last year. The joy wasn't as unfettered. The hearts weren't as carefree. Nothing was said at graduation about Sally Anders. She hadn't been a member of the senior class, and who wanted to mention her tragedy at a time like this?

But her presence was felt. Underneath the gaity and joy and uplift, and the turn of eyes to the future, the ghost of Sally Anders tossed and turned. For the first time in twelve years, Reginald Sawyer Sr. did not sit on the platform and sing a solo. For the first time in memory, the president of the senior class did not give a speech. And, among the gathered parents, relatives and friends, eyes and attention were not totally on the graduates. There were thoughts and whispers and shifting glances. "Is the killer sitting among us?" "Could it be Jerry Tuttle, looking so smug because his daughter won all those prizes?" "I've always wondered about Tom Raynor. I've never liked his eyes." "Hadn't Jud Prendergast always seemed a little too good to be true?" "I hear Jim Boardman has *Hustler* sent to his office, not his home." Friends were no longer friends because of the way they looked at each other. The unity of the town was shattered.

Monday June 15

JOURNAL OF DOROTHY MESKILL

I don't know what I'm doing today. I don't know what I'm thinking. I don't know what I'm feeling.

Today is graduation day. Today Ed and I attend the ceremonies on the Green, watch all the seniors, most of whom Ed has taught at one time or another, or directed in the school plays. Even those he doesn't know personally, he knows about. Ed's a student of human nature. He wants to know what makes people tick, why they do what they do, think what they think. His job gives him a great opportunity to study these things, and what he can't get firsthand, he tries to learn from talking to the student advisers. He makes notes about everything and is working on a book.

But I don't know this man. I suddenly discover, after all the years we've been married, that I don't know my husband. Suddenly, he frightens me. Suddenly I discover things about him I never knew before.

Let me write it down how it all happened while it's fresh in my mind, before we go to graduation.

It was around ten o'clock this morning. That's a guess, because I wasn't watching the clock. It was when Ed went up to the high school to pick up the rest of his things. I checked his closet to make sure he had a freshly pressed suit for the ceremonies. I look after those things. Ed is so sloppy. He's happiest going around in unpressed pants and shabby shoes. He doesn't believe clothes make the man. It's the man inside the clothes, he insists, and says who's the better man, Albert Einstein in his shapeless sweater, or Adolph Hitler in his shiny uniform? It's hard to argue against Ed, even if you know you're right.

So I take it upon myself not to debate with him, but look out for him, make sure he doesn't go to school in dungarees or forget to put on a tie. And I sorted through the closet to lay out the proper suit for him to wear, and I checked for anything that needed cleaning and pressing. And, at the back of the closet, tucked in a corner, I found a paper bag. I'd seen it before, as best I remember, and I assumed it contained old shoes or slippers or something. I'd just left it. But this time I took it out to see if anything in it needed looking after, and what was crammed into it was his old tweed sports jacket with the leather elbow patches, which I'd almost forgotten about.

It was wrinkled and crumpled, and all I thought was, He's ruining it. Why couldn't he at least put it on a hanger? Or give it to the Good Will if he didn't want it."

It was perfectly good, a couple of stains maybe, but all it needed was cleaning and pressing.

I checked the pockets before putting it aside for the cleaners, and I was stunned. In the right-hand side pocket was a pair of woman's panties! What on earth could those be doing there? I wondered. I mean, Ed isn't into collecting women's lingerie. And he couldn't be— Was he playing around?

Then I saw there were blood and grass stains on the panties, and I realized whose they were. They'd been worn by Sally Anders. They were the panties that were missing when she'd been found.

I knew Ed had been collecting statements, articles,

interviews, everything he could lay his hands on regarding the young girl's death—more of his research. "Sociology in the Raw," he called it. But how could he have gotten her panties? Even the police didn't know where they were.

I looked at the jacket and realized that its stains might also be blood. And suddenly I knew who'd killed Sally Anders. It was Ed.

But I couldn't believe it. Not Ed. There had to be some other reason for those panties being in his pocket.

I put it to him when he got back, showed him what he'd stuffed into his pocket, waited for him to explain.

I prayed for a flush of red in his face, an embarrassed, reluctant explanation of how he'd acquired a piece of evidence the police hadn't been able to find—the way he got all the other material for his research. Instead, he turned dead white and I knew, in that moment, that he was the one who had killed the girl.

He didn't deny it. He sat me down at the kitchen table and paced back and forth. Yes, he confessed, he'd done it. What I had to understand was the How and Why.

He patted my hands, white from gripping the table. "It's not what you think," he told me so earnestly I had to listen. He tore at his hair as he went back and forth, explaining the horror that had happened.

It had started, he said, back when Sally was a sophomore, in the drama club, and was trying out for a role in the school production of *Oklahoma!*, which he was directing. She'd been in his sociology class that year as well, and he sensed she was one of those girls who'd developed a "crush" on him. It's happened to him before, as he's told me, and I guess it happens to any attractive male teacher who has female pupils in his class. Some of them *do* develop "crushes." His problem, he said, lay in trying to ignore her obvious infatuation. He knew there'd be trouble if he cast her as Laurie in the *Oklahoma!* production. She'd take it as a sign her affection was reciprocated. But he had to be fair. She was best for the role, and he had to give it to her. And she'd done it well.

But she was enamoured of him. She was after him, arranging encounters, catching him alone in his room after school, begging rides, talking me down, building herself up, trying to make him believe his future and hers belonged together.

It's typical sophomoric fluff, "love conquers all." But how do you explain its fallacy to a child? For all his sociology, his study of human nature, Ed didn't know how. He tried, he said. God, how he tried! But such fixations are almost unrootable. He talked to her. He avoided her. He tried to make her see her future lay with boys her own age. But she had this father fixation. She was devoted to older men. And the older man was Ed. He couldn't make her let go.

And then it happened. She was baby-sitting just down the road. She knew I was out that evening, that Ed was home alone. And she phoned him. From the Parkers'. She had to see him. That's the way she put it. She was suicidal. She had a bottle of pills with her and she was going to swallow them all, right there, in the Parkers' house.

Ed was panicked. He hurried there to stop her, to talk her out of it. That was a mistake, he said. Once she had him there, she meant to settle matters. If he did not succumb to her, bend to her wishes, she would accuse him of trying to rape her. There he was, in the home where she was baby-sitting. How could he explain himself?

His remonstrations were in vain. She picked up the phone and dialed 911, the emergency number. That's when Ed panicked. There was a hammer on the counter and he hit her with it, to stop her from making the call. She fell, and he hung up the phone. Then he went to comfort her and try to explain to her. But he realized, in horror, that the hammer blow had killed her. She was dead on the floor.

Ed was frantic. He didn't know what to do. As he was telling it to me, the tears were streaming down his cheeks. He probably did it all wrong, he cried. Probably he should have called the police, told them the truth, and hoped it would be enough. But he also realized how bad it would look, that it would only be his word. There was no evidence, anywhere, to support him.

All he could think to do, he confessed to me, sobbing in remorse, was try to make it look as if she'd been raped and murdered by person or persons unknown. He carried her out and down into the field, he said. There, he hit her head some more with the hammer, to make it appear she'd been attacked, then stripped off her pants to give the impression the motive was rape.

Why he put her pants in his pocket, he didn't know. He didn't realize he'd done it. His only thought was to strip them off. He left her down in the field, threw the hammer into the bushes, and hurried back home. He didn't even remember he'd stuffed his sport coat in a bag in the back of the closet. All he wanted to do, he confessed, was hide the crime and bury his guilt.

Then he wept on my shoulder and pleaded with me to keep his secret with him. It wasn't as if, by keeping it secret, an innocent person would be convicted. Ed would speak out before he'd let anything like that happen.

But the mystery lay unsolved. The police had reached a dead end. No one would *ever* be punished.

It had been an accident. If the truth came out, what Sally had done, it would only sully her name further. And it would ruin him and me. There'd be a trial. The verdict would be manslaughter, a suspended sentence, but he'd have to resign his job and we'd have to find another life, somewhere else. And the cloud of Sally's death would follow us. It would be hard for him to get another position.

It would be best, he explained, if nothing were said. If we both kept quiet, nothing would happen. Our life would go on as it had.

He's right, of course. No purpose would be served by speaking out. Slowly, the fears engendered by Sally's death will dissipate. The townspeople will come to realize that, even though the mystery of her murder isn't solved, the danger of a recurrence isn't likely.

I've laid out his suit. We have to go to graduation now. Ed seems relieved and able to handle it. I don't know if I can.

Tuesday June 16

EDWARD MESKILL

It's after midnight now. Dorothy is asleep, troubled sleep, but asleep.

I suppose you know by now that the descriptive passages, the fill-ins in this account of Sally's death, were written by me.

I'm a sociologist and when all this happened, I thought I could put this terrible crime, the murder of Sally Anders, into a focus, into a picture of what goes on in a town when something horrible like that occurs. So I interviewed, I collected papers and reports, recollections of the people involved, the minutes and tapes of meetings. I thought it would make interesting reading.

Forget all that now. I've found Dorothy's journal and what she's written about discovering Sally's bloodstained panties in the pocket of my jacket.

I gave her a fast song and dance on that one, when she showed them to me. I didn't do a bad job either. My explanation sounds almost believable as I read what she wrote. And all of it was right off the top of my head! She

and a good bit frightened at getting the lead. She needed assurance, my steady hand—and I had champagne. She got giddy on the champagne, as I meant her to.

She wasn't the first little starlet I taught how to play love scenes to. She wasn't the first little girl who learned about womanhood from me. Little high-school girls who think they know what life's all about are great toys to practice sociology on. The tender phrase, the pseudo-reluctance to confess to their understanding souls the torments of one's own . . . Far older women than Sally fall eager prey to the "My wife doesn't understand me" line.

I don't mean I wasn't fond of Sally. She was as delightful as any of the others. But my charm, the charisma that held the others in thrall, wore thin with her. More and more she resisted my advances. More and more she wanted out of the whole thing.

And that's the fatal danger. Let a girl escape from the throes of your charm and you can't be sure how tight her lips will stay. When a woman stops viewing you as God, she ceases to worship. And where does it go from there? First, it's dismissal. Next you're a figment of her outgrown past. Then you become a joke. She laughs about you to her friends. And you're as surely cuckolded as if you'd been married.

Women talk! If there's one tried and sure thing about women, it is—they *talk*.

And a man in my position can't let that happen! You have to keep the little kittens quiet. They can scratch!

Sally Anders had never much liked it with me. Oh, we had our moments, particularly in the beginning, when she was awed by my superior age, experience, knowledge—my knowing how to satisfy a woman. Nobody, I pride myself, can satisfy a woman better than I.

It's what I rely on. It's the surefire method to keep a woman quiet.

It's kept Dorothy quiet. She's never asked questions before now. She's been convinced I'm a true and faithful husband.

But Sally Anders wasn't all that enthralled by my love-making. Deep down inside her, below the thrills, lay some kind of goddam puritanical conscience which told her it was wrong.

She'd been trying, almost from the beginning, to abort the relationship! I'd always had trouble soothing her. Now she was insistent. And I mean with a year of high school to go! Usually these things peter out *naturally* when the girls go off to college. It was just an experience. No hard feelings. A lasting fondness exists. The secret is forever kept.

But poor, dumb Sally was balky. She was turning me down, wanting to break it off, begging me to leave her alone. And what does a sociologist make of that? The girl was dangerous. If my charm had lost its power, what did I have to keep her from talking? A word to *anyone*, and I was finished!

I don't know if she saw it in the same light. She kept assuring me, even as she never wanted to see me again, that she'd never talk. But what are assurances? The power lay with her, not me. My future was at the mercy of her inadequate concern.

I knew she was going to be at the Parkers'. We had enough contact for that. I didn't tell her I was coming over. She would've locked the doors.

I came in on her, startled her. I wanted to reestablish the relationship. It was the only way I could be sure of her. And I wanted her as well. Let's face it, sex was involved—as it always is. Sally was a very young, attractive girl, and I like young, attractive girls. Even young girls if they *aren't* all that attractive. Never mind their faces, they have such lovely *bodies* at that age. I love Dorothy. She's not all that bright—not at all on my level intellectually—but she's good-hearted and well-intentioned. But she weighs thirty pounds more than she did when we married, and it shows. Never mind that stranger she feared was going to rape her. That's good for her ego, but she can't compare to a roomful of fifteen- and sixteen-year-old girls. God, I can't sit at the head of a class of girl students without picking out the ones I'd like to lay.

Most of the time, it's out of the question. But now and then, it can come about. You can make it actually happen. Those are the girls to remember!

But Sally was the one among them who wouldn't behave. She wanted out and I was afraid to let her out—afraid to lose control. And I walked in on her the night of May seventh and shocked the hell out of her.

I didn't mean to. My plan was to seduce her all over again. A little drink, a little talk, and a little sex—enough to make her want it some more.

She was outraged at my coming. She was outraged at the suggestion of a drink. She had children to mind. As for sex, it was as if we'd never had it together.

She told me to get out. Her voice was starting to keen to where she'd wake the children. I clapped a hand over her mouth to smother her cries, tried to soothe her. We wrestled, and I got aroused. I mean, we were struggling and I wasn't even thinking of sex at the moment, but suddenly that's all I could think of—what this struggling female in my arms was doing to me. And she *knew* I was aroused. And that made it worse. Because I had this craving for her and she wanted me out of the house.

She got free, but she knew what I was feeling, and she panicked. She shouldn't have panicked like that. If she only understood *men*, she'd have known what to do. But she ran to the phone instead. She tried to dial for help. I couldn't let her do that.

The hammer was there and I hit her with it. She fell, but she wasn't dead. She didn't die till later, till after I'd turned out the lights and carried her down into the field and raped her twice. I'm ashamed to have done that—raped her like that—but you have to understand what I was feeling. Once didn't even make a dent in my desires. I could've done it a third time. I would have, except the urge was no longer quite as strong as the worry about what was going to happen after.

She'd been going to report me to the cops when I hit her. What would she do now? She was still alive, because I'd've known it if I were raping a dead girl. She might have been comatose, but her body was still vibrant, if you know what I mean.

But she was dying. I think she was dying. Even if she weren't dying, she *had* to die. I couldn't let her tell on me.

So I stood over her. I think I'd pulled up my pants by then, and I hit her head again and again with the hammer. I had to make it look like brutality, like brutal rape, not just frustration.

I threw away the hammer where I knew it would be found, and I went home again, undressed and took a shower, and got ready for bed. I had to make it look natural when Dorothy got home. I remember now that I stuffed my jacket into that bag. It had her blood on it. The pants looked all right, except for one little stain, and I put them on again the next day. Funny how much I wanted to wear those pants to school the next day.

Of course, all hell broke loose over the murder. I was scared for a couple of days, especially when the police interviewed me to see if I'd heard screams from down the road while I was "correcting papers."

After that, though, I knew I was safe, and that's when I got the idea of collecting all this material and writing up the case.

Maybe I don't have to destroy all this data after all. Why can't I put it in a safe-deposit box to be opened after my death? That could be my legacy to the future: the solution of Crockford's Two Mysterious Unsolved Murders!

Correct that. One murder, one *disappearance*!

Dorothy can't be found murdered. No matter how cleverly it might be rigged, no matter how slickly it might be done, whenever a wife is murdered, the prime suspect, the one person the police are really going to dig into, is the husband!

I don't think the police in Crockford are especially bright, but I'm not a fool. Trying to get away with murdering my wife is more risk than I choose to run.

Dorothy has to disappear. And never be found.

Wednesday June 17

POLICE HEADQUARTERS (10:00 A.M.) PRESENT: Edward Meskill; Chief Herbert Hickey; Detective Sergeant Harry Dean.

EDWARD MESKILL
I want to report— I don't know how to say this, but my wife is missing.

CHIEF HICKEY
Missing? Your wife, Dorothy?

EDWARD MESKILL
Dorothy. She's gone. I don't know where.

CHIEF HICKEY
When? When did she disappear?

EDWARD MESKILL
I don't know. We went to graduation together Monday—

CHIEF HICKEY
How did she seem?

EDWARD MESKILL
As usual. I don't know what you mean.

CHIEF HICKEY
Was she bothered about anything? Was she upset at all?

EDWARD MESKILL
No, no. Everything was fine.

CHIEF HICKEY
Then what?

EDWARD MESKILL
Hugh Gibson, chairman of the Board of Education, had a cocktail party for the faculty in the gym of the high school when it was over. We went to that, had a drink or two, mingled, talked with people, and came home. . . .

CHIEF HICKEY
Any particular people Mrs. Meskill talked with?

EDWARD MESKILL
We kept together. I don't remember offhand whom we talked to, but I could come up with some names if it's important.

CHIEF HICKEY
Then what?

EDWARD MESKILL
We came home. I'd guess it was nine-thirty, ten o'clock. She was tired and went to bed, might have read—I don't know. I stayed up, had some work I wanted to do, and turned in a little after midnight, I guess. She was asleep in the next bed. As far as I knew, everything was fine.

CHIEF HICKEY
And then?

EDWARD MESKILL
Next morning I woke up around nine. No school anymore. Dorothy was up. Her bed was made. She's used to early rising, so I didn't think anything of that. She wasn't around the house, though. She usually makes breakfast and we eat together. But, as I say, school was over and I was up late and slept late.

So I got my own breakfast. I thought maybe she'd gone

shopping, except the car was in the yard. Maybe she was out playing tennis with the girls. She does that a lot. Except she hadn't left any note. But I didn't think anything of that because I'm usually at school and she doesn't have to leave notes.

I puttered around, mowed the grass, that sort of thing, and expected her home for lunch.

She didn't come.

I couldn't explain that. No note, no anything.

Not that I was worried. Most of the time I'm away all day and God knows what she does on her own. I'm not one of those husbands who wants an accounting. I figured she wasn't used to my being around the house, of any need to leave a message. She might have gone shopping in New Haven, or up in Hartford. She's a very capable woman. I didn't see anything to get alarmed about.

But she didn't come home for dinner. She didn't come home at all. I kept expecting her. When I got tired of waiting, I got something for myself.

Mind you, I wasn't too worried. I was sure there was a reasonable explanation. But I was starting to get a little bit alarmed. I mean, there didn't seem to be anything to be alarmed about. It's one of those things where some people start fearing the worst when somebody doesn't keep an appointment, but I know Dorothy. She's very capable, and I was sure, when she came back, she'd have a perfectly reasonable explanation as to where she'd been. As I say, she's not used to having me around and feeling the need to keep me apprised of everything she does.

But she didn't come home last night. Not for dinner, not after dinner.

I thought of calling you—calling the police. But I didn't really want to do that. I didn't want to bother you with something I was sure had a simple explanation. You people have enough problems on your hands.

Maybe her mother was sick and she had to go to her. Maybe it was a friend, something like that, where she got called away in a hurry and was so involved she didn't think to call. I don't know what I was thinking, except that she'd come home any minute and everything would be fine.

Well, she didn't come home at all.

I didn't want to be an alarmist and bother everybody, but I was worried. If only she'd left me a note! I mean, she'd got up in the morning, the way she'd always done, made the bed and all, and gone out somewhere, without taking the car. I didn't think she'd gone far. And if anything had happened to her, an accident or something, you people would have been coming to me. I wouldn't be coming to you.

But I got up this morning and she still wasn't back, and that was more than I could handle. I still think it's nothing serious, that there's a perfectly plausible explanation, but I don't know where my wife is, where she went, and I'm getting pretty damned nervous. It's a serious matter to report to the police that someone's missing, but this is my wife, and I want something done. I *want* her *found*!

CHIEF HICKEY

We understand that, Mr. Meskill. We certainly hope she can be. Can you think of any reason why she might have wanted to go away? Any family problems—difficulties between you?

EDWARD MESKILL

None whatsoever. We've been happily married for eleven years.

CHIEF HICKEY

She wouldn't have any reason to run away, or to commit suicide?

EDWARD MESKILL
Absolutely not!

CHIEF HICKEY
Do you play around with other women, Mr. Meskill?

EDWARD MESKILL
Certainly not! How *dare* you?

CHIEF HICKEY
Just looking for reasons why Mrs. Meskill might have wanted to go away.

EDWARD MESKILL
Wherever she went, it has nothing to do with me!

CHIEF HICKEY
You weren't playing around with Sally Anders?

EDWARD MESKILL
What?

CHIEF HICKEY
You don't, perhaps, try to seduce our young high-school girls? You don't sit in front of a class of girls and pick out the ones you'd like to . . . shall we say, *lay?*

EDWARD MESKILL

What? What are you saying? I don't know what you're talking about.

CHIEF HICKEY

We're talking about Sally Anders, Mr. Meskill, and what you did to her. Not what you told your wife you did to her, but what you yourself say you did to her.

EDWARD MESKILL

What *I* did to her? I didn't even know the girl!

CHIEF HICKEY

That's not what your wife tells us.

EDWARD MESKILL

My wife? Dorothy? You know where she is?

CHIEF HICKEY

She's in protective custody, Mr. Meskill. She discovered her journal was missing. It made her think, Mr. Meskill. And she realized the story you told her was a lie. You told her you made it look as if Sally Anders had been raped when, in actuality, Sally Anders *had* been raped.

Mrs. Meskill wasn't sleeping when you went to bed two nights ago, after your late-night's writing. She was lying awake and in terror, waiting for you to go to sleep yourself.

Then she hunted for her journal, knowing you'd hidden it as you'd hidden your bloodstained jacket and Sally

Anders's underpants. She found it, in the box of manu-
script papers you were collecting, along with your account
and your plans for her.

Mrs. Meskill didn't disappear yesterday morning, Mr.
Meskill. She came here.

We have a search warrant, sir. It just arrived, all nice
and legal. Detective Sergeant Dean and his men are going
through your house. They know where your jacket and
Sally's underpants are, where you've hidden the manu-
script you're working on, and your confession. Mrs. Meskill
has told us where they are.

I regret to have to inform you, Mr. Meskill, that we are
arresting you for the murder of Sally Anders and the
intent to murder your wife. Detective Sergeant Dean will
read you your rights. You may call a lawyer if you wish,
and I must warn you, in the meantime, that anything you
say hereafter can be used in a court of law against you. Do
you have any questions?

EDWARD MESKILL
May I see my wife?

CHIEF HICKEY
No.